ESPRESSOS, EGGNOGS, AND EVIL EXES

A Cape Bay Cafe Mystery Book 7

HARPER LIN

Harper Lin Books

Chapter 1

"10 . . . 9 . . . 8 . . . "

I chanted the numbers along with my friends and millions of strangers up and down the Eastern seaboard as the big crystal ball slowly made its descent over Times Square in New York City.

I was, fortunately, snug and cozy in my house, watching the ball drop on TV instead of in person. I'd done that before, and I was much happier cuddled up on the couch with my boyfriend Matt and a glass of champagne than I'd been standing in the freezing cold for hours on end just to watch some underwhelming pop stars lip sync—badly, in most cases—to their greatest hits while bouncing around the stage wearing either just enough to keep them on the right side of the law or a fur coat big enough that they looked more like a bear than a human being. After you'd suffered through that, the ball drop was exciting just because it meant you could finally go home.

" . . . 7 . . . 6 . . . 5 . . . "

I was enjoying this New Year's Eve for more reasons than just that it was spent surrounded by my friends, beside a roaring fire in the comfort of my own home. The year had been a long one. A tough one. A painful one. My entire life had fallen apart in the past year. I'd thought I was settled, working a stressful but fulfilling job and living with the man I thought I'd marry in the city that never sleeps. But then the man ran off with another woman, leaving me on the hook for an apartment I couldn't afford on my own. I should have picked up and moved home then, but I didn't. Not until my mother dropped dead at the way-too-young age of fifty-five, leaving my childhood home and the family business—Antonia's Italian Café —to me.

" . . . 4 . . . 3 . . . "

And then, somehow, I seemed to have taken up the hobby of solving murders in my small home town of Cape Bay on the coast of Massachusetts. The murders themselves had been shocking—Cape Bay's crime had been limited to petty theft and light vandalism. But this year there had been a series of murders, and I'd managed to get myself involved in investigating every single one of them. I'd solved them, but I was still looking forward to the fresh start of the new year. A new year I hoped would have as little death as possible—although if the sad little ficus in the corner of my living room finally gave up, I wouldn't be too torn up. Whatever other talents I had, caring for plants was not one of them.

"...2...1..."

What I did want in the new year was more of what I had right at that moment—my new boyfriend beside me, my friends gathered 'round, and my beloved Berger Picard dog sprawled across my lap. That, as far as I was concerned, was all I ever needed. Well, and maybe a good cup of coffee, but my espresso machine in the kitchen could handle that.

"...Happy New Year!"

I looked into Matt's warm, smiling brown eyes and tipped my head towards him. He bent his head and kissed me warmly, softly, tenderly. In spite of the room full of people, I was tempted to let the kiss go on and on. It was perfect. But then I remembered something.

I caught Matt looking confused out of the corner of my eye as I turned around to look at my friend Sammy, sitting on the other side of my small living room next to her maybe-boyfriend Ryan. She looked innocently back at me, maybe too innocently. She and Ryan had been flirting for months now, and were all pretty sure they were together, but she still stubbornly denied that anything was going on between them despite all the evidence to the contrary. I had hoped that I'd be able to catch them sharing the traditional

New Year's kiss, but I was either too late or they hadn't done it. Based on the looks on their faces, I suspected I'd missed it.

I caught our friend and coworker Rhonda's eye she shook her head slightly and shrugged. She hadn't caught what Sammy and Ryan did or didn't do either. Then Rhonda tipped her head towards the fourth couple in our little quartet. It was Sammy's best friend Dawn and her boyfriend of the moment, Jack or Jay or Jason—something like that. I couldn't keep up with them, but it didn't really matter because he'd be replaced by someone new within a couple of weeks. But for now, they were all over each other. All. Over. Each. Other. Right there in the middle of my living room with the rest of us looking on—or looking away uncomfortably.

Rhonda nudged her husband and pointed towards Dawn. He waggled his eyebrows at her and grinned. She laughed. He laughed too, which made Rhonda laugh harder. Soon the two of them were lost in a giggle fit, which spread to me and then Matt, and then Sammy and Ryan. Even with all six of us cracking up, it still took Dawn and Jared or Jaden or Jacob a few seconds to look up.

"What?" Dawn asked, wiping at the corner of her mouth.

Jacques or Javier or Jamiroquai stared at us blankly—he wasn't the sharpest tool in the shed—

when we all laughed harder as we saw the smear of dark red lipstick around his mouth.

Dawn at least caught on and started laughing too. "Oh, honey," she said and licked her thumb to rub the lipstick off his face. It only made it redder. Dawn shrugged and gave up. Her boyfriend looked completely unconcerned as he slugged back his glass of champagne.

At least that reminded me that I had planned to use the champagne for a toast.

"A toast!" I said, harnessing my giggles as I held my champagne glass up. I tried to sit up straighter, too, but Latte, proving nothing got in the way of my dog and his sleep, remained stubbornly sprawled across my lap.

At least everyone paid attention to me anyway and raised their glasses in the air, even Dawn's boyfriend whose glass was empty.

"To new friends—" I began, gesturing towards Sammy and Rhonda. "—and old—" I gestured to Matt. "To new experiences and coming home again. And to fresh starts. Because I think we could all use one after last year." I paused again and looked around at my friends—the people I considered my new family. Well, except for Jackson or Jacopo or Jafar. "Cheers."

"Cheers!" my friends said.

I clinked my glass against Matt's and then Rhonda's since they were the only two I could reach, and drank my champagne down. It was a little warmer than I would have liked—I poured it too early—but it was still bubbly and tasty.

"That's good champagne," Dawn said. "You have any more?"

"Nope. But there's still plenty of eggnog," I said.

"Ooh, that was good, too," Dawn said. Then she narrowed her eyes at me. "Wait, you mean the one with or without the rum?"

I narrowed my eyes back. "That depends on how you're planning to get home."

For a second, she looked panicked, even though she lived less than a mile away and I was pretty sure she'd walked over. Habit, I guessed.

"I'll make sure she gets home," Ryan said.

Sammy flashed him a smile.

"Ryan's taking me," Dawn said, as if she thought I hadn't heard him.

"To your apartment," Ryan said quickly. "I mean, I'll make sure you get back to your apartment okay. You and—" He waved his hand in the direction of Dawn's date like he couldn't remember his name either. "—him. Assuming he's going back to your place, I mean."

"Oh, he is," she nodded with a smug look on her face and went to sip her empty glass of champagne. "Ugh. I forgot." She held it out towards whatever his name was. "Babe, could you get me some more?"

"I'll get it!" Sammy said, hopping up quickly and

grabbing the glass from Dawn's hand. I had a feeling she was more interested in making sure Dawn didn't drink too much than in saving the boyfriend of the month the trouble of getting up. She picked up the empty plastic drink cup from the table next to Dawn, too. "Anyone else?"

"I'll take some," Matt said.

I elbowed him in the ribs.

"What?"

"You don't need Sammy to get your drinks for you. You're the co-host tonight. You don't have your guests get your drinks for you."

"She offered," he protested.

"That doesn't mean you have to accept."

He gave me a crooked smile. "Well, my *girlfriend* could always get me some."

"I would, but—" I said, and gestured at Latte still sprawled across my lap. As if by magic though, he decided to take that moment to reposition himself— on Matt's lap instead of mine.

"Problem solved!" Matt said.

I shook my head at him as I stood up. "Anyone else?"

"A glass of water?" Rhonda's husband Dan asked.

"Sure thing. Anyone else?"

"Just make sure Sam gets me the eggnog with the rum, okay?" Dawn asked.

"Of course." With no one else making any

requests and Sammy already disappeared around the corner, I headed for the kitchen.

When I got there though, Sammy wasn't ladling eggnog into Dawn's cup. Instead, she was staring at her phone, her face white as a ghost's.

Chapter 2

"WHAT'S WRONG?" I asked.

The way Sammy was staring at her phone, I knew that whatever had upset her had to do with what she saw on it. We still had the TV on in the other room, so I knew it couldn't be some horrible event somewhere in the world. Her phone hadn't rung, so no one had called her to deliver bad news. A text? But how bad could it be if someone was texting her to tell her?

"Sammy?"

She looked up, startled. "Fran! I, uh, I didn't see you there," she said hurriedly as she shoved her phone into her pocket.

I abandoned the glasses I'd brought into the kitchen on the counter and took a step closer to her. "What's wrong?"

"Nothing! Why do you ask?" Even if I hadn't seen the look on her face moments before, the strained tone of her voice and the too-bright expression on her face would have been dead giveaways that something was going on.

"Because I saw the look on your face when I walked in here and how fast you shoved your phone in your pocket and plastered that fake smile on your face when you saw me. You're obviously upset about something."

"It's no big deal." She shook her head and kept smiling blankly.

"Sammy?" I used the same tone I used with Latte when he was hiding a chew toy he didn't want me to remember he had. But Sammy didn't try to distract me with sad puppy dog eyes. Instead she just kept looking at me with scared blue ones like she hoped I'd give up. She was wrong. I took another step towards her and reached out to brush her arm supportively. "Whatever it is, you can tell me."

She stared at me for a few more seconds then exhaled like she'd been holding her breath. "I got another text from Cheryl."

"Ryan's ex?"

She nodded.

"She's still doing that?"

She nodded again.

I made a face. The Cheryl in question had shown up in town a few weeks earlier, shortly before Christmas, and had set up camp in my café, the better to harass Sammy. After I kicked her out and told her not to come back, she'd switched to texting Sammy. A lot. When Sammy first told me about it, back on Christmas Eve, she'd already gotten dozens of messages in just a week's time. She'd told me Cheryl sent them all day, every day. And she signed them all "Love, Cheryl." It was definitely creepy. And I was ashamed to admit that between the holidays themselves and not seeing Sammy as much with the café on limited hours because of them, I'd basically forgotten about the texts after she told me.

"Was it bad?"

She dug her phone out of her pocket, unlocked it, and thrust it towards me.

I took it and looked at the last message to come in.

Happy New Year! Hope you and Ry-Ry are having a great time at your party! You're so lucky to have so many great friends! Love, Cheryl PS—Your apartment is SO cute!!! xxxx

A little chill ran down my spine and not because my kitchen was a little drafty.

I started scrolling up through the previous messages from Cheryl. There were a lot of them. A *lot*. A frightening amount. I didn't read each one, but all the ones I did had the same overly-cheerful, creepily-personal tone. Too many of them mentioned Sammy's clothing or hairstyle, or commented on what she'd done that day.

I looked up from the phone. "Does Ryan know about this?"

She shook her head.

"Sammy, you have to tell him!"

"No. I can't."

"You *can't?* Why not?"

She shrugged.

"He's the reason why she's harassing you. Maybe he can do something to get her to stop. And if he can't, he's a cop. He can get her to stop that way."

She shook her head again.

"Why *not?*" I felt almost childish demanding an answer from her like that, like I may as well stomp my foot and pout about it.

She stared at the floor and wrapped a lock of blonde hair tightly around her finger. Finally, she answered. "I don't want to be that kind of girl."

"What kind of girl?" I didn't know what she meant. The kind of girl who sticks up for herself? The kind who doesn't let herself get walked all over? The kind who doesn't end up as the true story some creepy TV movie is based on?

"The high maintenance kind who always has some kind of drama."

"Oh, Sammy." I went to give her a hug but had only just stepped towards her when Dawn walked in. Sammy grabbed her phone away from me and shoved it back in her pocket. Something about it made me feel even more uneasy than I already did.

"What's taking so long?" Dawn announced, loud enough that I was pretty sure my neighbors could hear her.

"Just got distracted chit-chatting," Sammy said quickly. She picked up one of the cups she'd brought in and ladled it full of eggnog. The non-alcoholic, I noticed. She handed it to Dawn who immediately slugged it back.

"Bleh!" Dawn stuck her tongue out like she'd tasted something disgusting. "You gave me the wrong one!" She dumped it out in the sink—without rinsing it down—then refilled her cup from the other bowl. She picked up the bottle of rum next to the bowl and dumped a couple of healthy glugs into the already boozy eggnog.

"You know you could have just added rum to the first cup," I said, stepping over the sink and turning the faucet on to clear away the milky residue.

Dawn thought for a second. "Yeah, I could have." She shrugged. "Oh well." She added another hefty dose of rum to her cup. I didn't envy her the hangover she would certainly have the next morning.

"Hey, we're going to take off," Rhonda said, poking her head into the room.

"Have to go pick up the boys?" I asked. Rhonda's two teenage sons had been invited to ring in the New Year with a friend whose mother had apparently been adamant that no one but the people who lived in her house would be spending the night. Rhonda had already entertained us with an impression of the woman earlier in the night.

"Yep. We're already pushing it to get them by

twelve-thirty. Did I tell you she originally wanted everyone picked up by twelve-fifteen? Why have them over if you're going to kick them all out ASAP?" She sighed. "Anyway, thanks for having us." She hugged me, then Sammy, then Dawn. "Coats?" she asked.

"Oh, I'll get them." I scurried out of the kitchen and through the living room to what had, for most of my life, been my grandparents' bedroom. I'd been living alone in the house for nearly six months now and still hadn't gotten myself moved into it. I'd finally cleaned it out, but hadn't yet managed to get much further in the process. I told myself it was because I was so busy with the café.

I came out a moment later with Rhonda and Dan's coats, only to find the rest of my guests gathered around the door too. "You're leaving already?"

Ryan looked over at Dawn who was leaning heavily on what's-his-name. He, in turn, was barely keeping himself vertical. "It's for the best," Ryan said.

I nodded wordlessly, handed Rhonda and Dan their coats and went back for the others.

It had been unseasonably warm for the few days, but even unseasonably warm on the coast, in Massachusetts, in the middle of the night, in January was pretty cold. It took a good several minutes for everyone to get themselves, and then Dawn and her escort all bundled up.

As Ryan tried to hold Dawn upright and still so that Sammy could button her coat for her, Matt grinned at him. "And you thought you were going to get away with not dealing with any drunks for New Year's."

Ryan rolled his eyes.

"I can't believe Mike got stuck working the holiday *again*," I said, holding Dawn's arm as Sammy struggled to shove Dawn's gloves onto her hands. "You'd think that if you worked Christmas Eve, you'd get New Year's Eve off." Our friend Mike was a detective in the Cape Bay Police Department had had somehow gotten stuck working patrol on both holidays despite outranking and having more time with the department than most of the force, including Ryan.

Ryan shrugged. "I don't know, but I'm not complaining."

I wondered what was going on. Ryan had thought that Mike volunteered to work Christmas Eve, but that hadn't sounded right to me. Not when he had kids, or when his family was celebrating the holiday out at his in-laws' cabin in the mountains a couple hours away. He'd gone out there to spend Christmas Day with them, but had come right back, leaving the rest of his family there. In fact, I was pretty sure they were still there. It was strange. I hoped him having to work the holiday shifts wasn't some kind of punishment the department was doling out to him. His last case *had* been particularly rocky though. Maybe he was just doing it for the overtime pay though.

"Alright, we better get these two out of here," Ryan said, moving Dawn in the direction of the door.

Beside me, Sammy's cell phone blinged and she tensed up almost imperceptibly. I glanced at Ryan, but he didn't seem to have noticed.

"You'll make sure she gets home okay, won't you?" I asked Ryan.

"Yeah, but that's all I'm doing," he said. "I'm not responsible for her after she walks through that door though."

For a second, I was horrified. Then Matt leaned over. "He means Dawn."

"Oh! No, I don't expect you to babysit Dawn!"

Sammy had told me stories about Dawn's drunken exploits—going back out to party some more after Sammy dropped her off at home being the most common one. Dawn was fun, but sometimes she was a little *too* much fun. And she definitely wasn't someone you could control.

As if to prove that, Dawn laughed from outside. We all turned to see her and her, uh, gentleman friend chasing each other around my front yard. The girl had been barely able to stand while we got her bundled up and now she was running around my tree root covered front yard in the dark with no problem.

"I meant Sammy. You'll make sure Sammy gets home okay, right?" I said, redirecting my attention away from the game of tag in my front yard and back to Ryan.

"Of course!" He slung his arm around Sammy's shoulders, initiating just about the most physical contact I'd ever seen between the two of them. I couldn't be sure in the dim light of my foyer, but I thought Sammy's cheeks turned ever-so-slightly pinker at his touch.

"And I don't just mean walk her home. Make sure she gets inside all right, okay? Have her flash the lights or something when she gets in?"

The maybe-blush seemed to intensify on Sammy's cheeks and Ryan started to look bashful. I didn't care though. Cheryl's text made me nervous.

"I'll make sure she's safe and sound."

"I just mean, a single woman living alone—"

"I think he's got it, Franny," Matt said, interrupting me.

"I just—"

"He's got it."

I looked at Sammy. "Text me when you get home, okay?"

"I will."

There was another loud laugh from outside. We looked out to see Dawn launching herself onto her date's back. Or trying to, anyway. What she actually did was fall off the side, then get up and walk several feet away to attempt it again with a running start.

"We should go," Ryan said quickly.

We hugged our goodbyes—well, except for Matt and Ryan who just sort of slapped each other on the back. When Sammy hugged me, she whispered in my ear, "Thanks for looking out for me." Before I could say anything in return, she was on her way out the door towards Ryan who was using his best cop-breaking-up-a-crowd voice at Dawn and the guy toting her around on his back—she'd finally managed to get up there after all.

"Okay! Let's go! Come on guys! Time to move on!" He gradually herded them toward the sidewalk and down the street. Sammy gave me a last little wave. I waved back, my brain full of concern about the Cheryl situation.

"I'm sure Ryan will keep an eye on her," Matt said quietly. "And maybe some other body parts too."

"Matty!" I swatted at him, but he jumped back out of my reach.

"What? It's what I plan on doing with you!" This time when I tried to swat at him, he grabbed my hand and pulled me close to him. "You got a problem with that?"

I made a face like I was thinking about it and he pulled me even closer, right up against his warm, strong chest. "No, I don't think I do."

Chapter 3

A HIGH-PITCHED NOISE slowly pierced my consciousness. It started and stopped, started and stopped, started and stopped. Through the fog of sleep, I kept hoping it would stop for good, but every time I thought it had, it started right back up again. Maybe even a little louder. My sleep-addled brain didn't know what it was, but was pretty sure it didn't want to deal with it.

Something cold and wet touched my face. Then something warm and wet.

"Hi Latte," I murmured, reluctantly reaching one hand out of the snuggly warmth of the sheets and out into the cold air to scratch his head.

When I stopped, he nudged my hand again. I scratched his head again. Then the high-pitched noise started again and I realized it was Latte whining for food. Or to go out. Or maybe both. Probably both. I groaned. One hand was bad enough. I did not want to expose my whole body to the chill of my bedroom.

Latte whined again. I wondered how Matt could possibly not hear that. Of course, there was the possibility that he could hear it and was just ignoring it in hopes that I would get up and take care of it. Just like I was hoping he would.

Another whine and I gave in. I slung my legs out of the bed and sat up. My room was the bedroom I'd grown up in and it had always been cold and a little drafty during the winter. I didn't remember it bothering me when I was a kid though. I slid my feet into my slippers to save them from the cold floor and looked at the time on my phone. It was just before seven. The sun wasn't even up yet. You'd think he could have given me a break since it was New Year's, but nope. He was up even earlier than usual.

I grabbed my robe as I headed for the stairs. Latte ran straight for his food bowl, so I filled it up and sat down at the kitchen table, hoping the food was all he wanted even though I knew it wasn't. Sure enough, as soon as he was done, he walked over and looked at me with those puppy dog eyes. "All right, you win." I scratched his head and made my way back upstairs to get myself dressed enough to take him for a walk. On my way past the thermostat, I cranked the heat up. I was going to be frozen to the core by the time we got back and I wanted to at least have the luxury of walking back into a toasty warm house. Maybe I'd even get lucky and Matt would light a fire for me.

A few minutes later, fully clothed in my very warmest sweats, I stood in front of my commercial-grade home espresso machine. The Amaro family didn't mess around when it came to coffee. I pulled more shots of espresso than I probably should have, but I was tired and needed the fortification. On a whim, I grabbed the leftover eggnog from the refrigerator and steamed that to add on top of the espresso in my very large insulated cup. I was surprisingly pleased with the finished product even though—or maybe because—it was more espresso than eggnog.

Latte, knowing my morning routine better than any dog had a right to, was hovering by the front door. I slipped on my heavy winter coat and reached in the pockets for my gloves. Which were missing. I checked my lighter coat and my purse. Nothing. I looked down at Latte who stared back in full innocent puppy dog mode. I sighed. Cold hands it would be. I pulled my warm woolen hat down low over my ears and wrapped my scarf around my neck. I grabbed my cup, silently cursed its outstanding insulation that kept all the heat in and allowed none of it to reach my soon-to-be frozen hands, hooked Latte onto his leash, and headed outside.

I was sufficiently tired that I just let Latte lead me wherever he wanted to go. Not that I usually made him follow a strict path, but today I was especially laid back about it. If he wanted to walk through the park, fine. If he wanted to turn down a street we didn't usually go down, no problem. If he wanted to wander down a path worn through some back yards, I was game. He seemed to have a mission, sniffing the ground as he walked, so I let him pursue it. We walked all over town. Through my neighborhood, up to Main Street, past my café, back down another residential street, around a couple of corners. The town was exceptionally quiet, even for an early morning. Everyone was tucked inside their houses, enjoying the last opportunity of the holiday season to sleep late . . . or sleeping off the night before. Everyone but me.

My coat and hat and large cup of coffee were keeping me warmer than I'd expected, which I was grateful for as Latte didn't show any signs of slowing down. It probably helped that I kept whichever hand wasn't currently holding the coffee buried in a pocket. And the hand that was holding it was as far into my sleeve as I could manage.

After a while, I decided it was time to head back home. To be honest, I wasn't even totally sure where we were at the moment, but it was Cape Bay—it wouldn't be hard to figure it out once I got Latte back to the road. We were currently on one of his side explorations through some backyards. "Come on, Latte," I said, tugging at his leash to try to get him to turn back towards the road. As far as I could tell, he didn't even notice. "Latte!" He didn't even flinch, just strained at the leash like he was determined to find whatever it was he was looking for. I sighed and gave in. I'd let him explore a little bit longer. I still had a couple of ounces of coffee in my cup.

He trotted resolutely down the walking path, dragging me along behind him. Then, suddenly, he veered off and tried to head into someone's backyard. "Latte! No!" He kept pulling. "Latte!" Still nothing. "Latte!" I decided that my New Year's resolution was going to have to be to look into obedience training. He began to bark. "Latte! Hush!" I whisper-yelled at him. He didn't care. I decided it was better to just follow him into the yard than to wake up the whole neighborhood's attention with his barking.

I looked around as Latte dragged me towards whatever his prize was and recognized Ryan's car sitting in front of one of the houses—the house Latte seemed intent on dragging me to.

Ryan's was a hard-to-forget vehicle. One of those odd, boxy SUVs that nobody claimed to like but a lot of soccer moms seemed to drive. Matt teased Ryan about it pretty regularly. Ryan defended himself by saying he'd gotten it dirt cheap.

There was a big black trash bag laying in the middle of Ryan's yard and I realized that must have been what was drawing Latte's attention. Nothing like garbage to get a dog excited early in the morning.

Latte trotted towards the trash bag. It was definitely what he was going for. Why there was a trash bag lying in the middle of Ryan's backyard, I didn't know. I hoped some critter hadn't gotten into it and dragged it out there, probably tearing it open in the process, and making it easy for my dog to access whatever stinky, smelly leftover food was probably in it.

Something about the trash bag didn't look right though. Namely that it wasn't a trash bag. It was a black winter coat. The thought flashed through my brain that someone must have been pretty drunk the night before to abandon their coat outside.

But they hadn't abandoned it. As I got closer, I realized there were jeans and a pair of boots with the coat. Also not abandoned. So then I wondered how drunk you had to be to lay down and go to sleep in the middle of someone's backyard in January. Whoever it was was lucky they had that warm coat on.

I wrapped Latte's leash around my hand, forcing him to stay closer as I moved forward.

I spotted a shock of blonde hair and my stomach clenched. It wasn't—it couldn't be. And then as quickly as the thought that it was Sammy popped into my head, I realized it wasn't her. The hair wasn't the right shade of blonde and it wasn't long enough. But I knew someone else who had that shade of blonde hair. And she had no business being in Ryan's backyard.

"Cheryl!" I yelled as I stomped over. The way she was laying on her stomach, it looked like she was spying on the house. I wondered if she'd been there all night or had just arrived early this morning to watch what he was up to.

Cheryl didn't move, which made me even angrier. Like she thought she could just play possum and I wouldn't notice her. "Cheryl!" I yelled again, standing right over her. Still nothing. Despite my anger, I had a flicker of worry that she really had fallen asleep there or had passed out. Even with the coat, a whole night outside would give you a chill.

I bent down and shook her shoulder. "Cheryl!" No response. I pushed her over onto her back and froze. She hadn't fallen asleep. Her eyes were open, staring up at the sky. Her face was completely slack and covered with little speckled bruises. And her neck—

The next thing I knew, someone was screaming.

Chapter 4

THE SCREAMING DIDN'T STOP until I finally realized it was coming from me. By that time, Latte was going crazy barking, and I'd woken up half the neighborhood. At least, that's what I had to assume by the number of people who had suddenly appeared. Two of those people were Ryan and Sammy. They both came running towards me.

"What's going on? What happened?" Ryan asked. He pulled me away from Cheryl's body and pushed me towards Sammy. I held my breath as he bent to check Cheryl's pulse, hoping that, despite all the signs to the contrary, maybe she was still alive. When he closed her eyes, I knew she wasn't. "Sammy, go get a sheet and my cell phone from inside the house," he said. "Fran, go up there with her. Take Latte."

That was when I realized I must have dropped his leash. "Come on, Latte." I patted my thigh as I followed Sammy back towards Ryan's house. For the first time that morning, Latte actually listened to me.

"Everybody go back inside your houses! There's nothing to see here!"

I stayed on the patio while Sammy went inside. She came back a minute later with the sheet and cell phone. Ryan met her partway across the lawn and took both items from her. He covered Cheryl's body with the sheet, then dialed the phone and held it to his ear. Sammy and I leaned against the house, Latte sitting obediently between us. Neither of us spoke.

After a minute or two on the phone, Ryan walked back up to the patio.

"What—what happened?" I stammered. "Was— was she—" I struggled to ask the question even though the answer was obvious. Some part of me just hoped Ryan would say that she had a medical condition that made her face and neck explode in bruises just before she dropped dead.

"The police will take our statements when they get here. We shouldn't discuss anything before then."

"But you are the police," I said stupidly.

"Not on this case, I'm not."

It made sense in some part of my brain—it's probably not looked highly upon to investigate the body that shows up in your yard—but another part of my brain didn't see what the problem was. A cop is a cop, regardless of the case, right?

The sound of sirens distracted me. Once the police got here, we'd be able to talk about it.

Mike Stanton, our friend and detective in the Cape Bay Police Department, was the first to come around the corner of the house, followed by another uniformed officer who I recognized vaguely but didn't know the name of.

"Leary, what've we got?" Mike said, barely breaking stride as he walked past Ryan.

Ryan jogged to catch up with him. They spoke quietly, so I couldn't hear them, but I imagined it was something along the lines of "Fran found my ex-girlfriend strangled to death in my backyard and started screaming so loud that it woke up me and my current girlfriend—"

I turned to look at Sammy. "You spent the night here!"

She blushed a bright red and looked down at her feet which, I noticed, were wearing what looked to be Ryan's shoes. The sweatpants she was wearing were also Ryan's, at least if "Buffalo Police"—Ryan's previous employer—was any indication. Her coat was her own at least. Before either of us could say anything, Mike and Ryan walked back over.

"Sammy, you're going to talk to Simmons," he said, pointing at the other uniformed officer. "Fran, you're coming with me."

The paramedics passed us on their way to the body as I followed Mike around the front of the house and in the direction of his patrol car. I swallowed hard as he opened the back door.

"C'mon, Latte," he said, gesturing for him to hop in. Again, he was mysteriously obedient and hopped right in. I moved more slowly, reluctant to find myself in the back seat of a police car. "What are you doing?" Mike asked as he shut the door in my face. "You're up front." I must have looked as confused as I felt. "It's warm in here and you can't be within earshot of Sammy while you give your statement."

"What about Ryan?"

"I'll talk to him when I'm done with you." Mike opened the passenger side door for me. "Sorry about the mess." He swiped some of the energy drink cans and fast food wrappers off the seat and onto the floor-boards. I was surprised by how messy it was. I didn't think of Mike as a messy guy, but his car looked like he'd been living in it.

Once I was situated inside, Mike walked around and got in the driver's side. He pulled his gloves off and grabbed a little notebook out of his coat pocket. "You wanna tell me what happened?"

I gave him the rundown of seeing what I thought was a trash bag in the yard, realizing it was Cheryl, rolling the body over, and screaming.

"What were you doing in Ryan's backyard?"

"Taking Latte for a walk."

At the mention of his name, Latte smashed nose

up to the divider between the front and back seats. I wished I'd brought some dog biscuits for him.

"Through Ryan's backyard?" Mike asked, clearly doubting my story.

I told him how we'd just been wandering, realizing as I said it that it may not sound entirely convincing. My dog got me up early, so I didn't pay attention to where we were going? Great explanation, Fran. Not that I had anything to be afraid of, but talking to the police after finding an apparently murdered body would put anybody on edge. Especially with the amount of caffeine I'd had.

Mike didn't seem fazed by it though, just scribbling some notes in his notebook. At least until he looked at my hands. "Nervous?"

I held my hands up and realized they were shaking violently. "Just cold, I think. Or too much caffeine." I held up my coffee cup. "I had a lot."

For a second, Mike gazed longingly at the large cup. He was a caffeine addict if I'd ever seen one. And I noticed his car's cupholder was empty.

"I'd offer you some, but it's empty," I said, jiggling it back and forth so he could hear the few remaining drops sloshing around.

"You just gotta close Antonia's on holidays, don't you, Fran? How am I supposed to get my caffeine fix?"

"Gas station?" I offered, almost traitorously. But even if I was suggesting one of my customers go somewhere else for coffee, I was at least glad that we seemed to have moved on from the conversation about the dead body.

"I'd rather live on these Beast energy drinks than drink that stuff."

"How'd you get stuck working New Year's Eve *and* Christmas Eve, anyway?"

He didn't answer for a second, then he shrugged. "Luck of the draw, I guess."

"Bad luck! Shouldn't you get preference since you've been there for so long?"

He tapped his pen on his notepad a few times, apparently ignoring me. "Did Ryan and Sammy seem surprised to see Cheryl's body in the backyard?"

I stared at him for a second, startled to be back to the official conversation. "Well, yeah."

"'Well, yeah?'" Mike repeated. "Did you actually notice that they were surprised or are you assuming that was their reaction based on how you felt?"

At first, I tried to really remember what their reactions had been. I had been so shocked, did I even look at them when they came outside? Did I actually see them come out or had I just noticed them when they were already outside? It seemed obvious that they had been surprised, but did I remember seeing that on their faces? And then I realized what Mike was really asking.

"You can't think one of them had something to do with it!"

Mike drummed on his notepad.

"Mike!"

He raised his eyebrows.

"Mike!"

"It has nothing to do with what I think, Fran. Ryan's ex-girlfriend's body was found in his backyard. His ex-girlfriend who had been harassing his new girlfriend."

I gasped. "You know about that?"

He looked at me curiously. "We had a call to Antonia's before Christmas about her refusing to leave the café. I believe you were the caller."

"Oh that!"

Mike raised an eyebrow. "What did you think I was talking about?"

"That. I just didn't think you would know about it since you weren't the one who responded to the call."

The other eyebrow went up. "I hope you're not hiding something from me, Fran."

My heart raced as he held my gaze, and not in the good way it did when Matt stared into my eyes. Sammy had begged me not to tell anyone about the text messages Cheryl had been sending her, but that was before Cheryl showed up dead. It couldn't possibly matter now, could it? Unless it made it look like Sammy had a motive. But in that case, wouldn't it be better if he found out now rather than later?

"Fran?"

I clenched my still-trembling hands in my lap and

stared at them. It must have been the caffeine making them shake more than the cold.

"If there's anything I should know, it's better that I find out now."

I clenched my hands tighter. "That wasn't the only thing Cheryl was doing."

"Okay."

I watched my knuckles turn white. "Sammy told me about it in confidence and I don't want to break her trust."

"What else was Cheryl doing, Fran? I need to know."

I took a deep, slow breath and hoped Sammy would forgive me. "She was texting her."

"Cheryl was texting Sammy?"

I nodded. "A lot. Several times a day. And they were . . . creepy. She signed them all 'love, Cheryl.' And they commented on what Sammy was doing, things she shouldn't have known about, like Sammy and Ryan going to his parents' house for Christmas. Or her coming to my house for New Year's. She even said Sammy's apartment was cute. How would she know that?"

"And you think Cheryl was doing this to intimidate Sammy?"

"Why else would she be doing it?"

Mike shrugged. "I'm just trying to get your perspective on the situation."

"Then, yes. I think she was doing it to intimidate Sammy. I can't think of any other reason why."

"Because Sammy was replying?"

"She wasn't though! She told me she wasn't and she showed me the messages on her phone. She never replied."

Mike nodded and scribbled in his notebook, then tapped at it again. He asked me a few more questions about my explanation of the events of the morning—what time I left my house, exactly what position Cheryl's body had been in, how I knew it was her—then let me go. "If you remember anything else, you have my number," he said. "Oh, and I may need you to come down to the station in the next couple of days just to sign an official statement. Just a routine thing."

"Got it," I replied, reaching for the door handle. "Just let me know." I had just popped the door open when he stopped me.

"One more thing, Fran."

I paused, my hand still on the door.

"You never said whether you actually saw that Ryan and Sammy were surprised to see Cheryl's body or if you just assumed that they were."

I looked at him. He looked at his notepad. I didn't know whether it was a detective technique or if he didn't want to see the look in my eyes at the insinuation that my friends—his friends!—may have had something to do with Cheryl's death. I wanted to swear up and down that they had been every bit as shocked as I was to see her body lying there, but the truth was that I wasn't sure. "I don't know," I said, my voice as cold as the wind outside. "I was too busy screaming about the dead body I'd just found to study the expressions on the faces of everyone who came outside to see what was going on."

"Thanks. That's all I wanted to know."

I glared at him for a few more seconds, but he didn't even seem to notice, so I got out of the car, retrieved Latte from the back seat, and went to find Sammy.

I found her still around the back, leaning up against the house. "You done giving your statement?" I asked.

She nodded.

"Are you okay?"

She nodded again.

I put my hand on her shoulder.

"I can't believe she's dead," she said quietly.

"I know. It's—it's hard to believe."

"Another murder."

"You know, my New Year's resolution was to not get involved in any more murders and the first thing I do on New Year's Day is to find a body."

Sammy laughed. The sound burst out of her more loudly than was probably appropriate with a woman's dead body laying less than thirty feet away from us. The crime scene techs had just arrived and were getting ready to photograph the scene, but stopped to stare at us.

I smiled weakly and waved in their direction. "Nothing to see here, don't mind us, nothing going on over here," I said so quietly that only Sammy could hear. She laughed again, but kept it quieter this time. The crime scene techs turned back to their job.

"You know, I'm sorry you found her, but I'm glad you're here, Fran. This is scary. That officer was asking me questions like he thought I had something to do with her dying."

I couldn't tell her that Mike had asked me the same kind of questions, so I just rubbed her arm supportively. "You have Ryan, too."

She shook her head. "They won't let us near each other. Not until we've given our official statements."

"But—you just talked to them."

"They said we have to go down to the station and give written statements."

My stomach clenched in fear. Between the questions we'd both gotten, her being kept away from Ryan, and needing to go to the station to give her statement, I was worried for her. I put my arm around her shoulders and took a breath. "Sammy, you don't think you need a lawyer, do you?"

She looked at me with wide blue eyes and shook her head. "No—no. No. I didn't do anything. I don't need a lawyer if I didn't do anything, do I?"

"I—I don't know." Part of me thought it would be

a good idea, just based on the situation, but part of me thought it might make her look guilty and that was the last thing she needed right now. They already seemed suspicious enough of her. Before I could think about it any more, the officer who had arrived with Mike—Simmons—popped around the corner of the house.

"Miss Eriksen? It's time to go down to the station."

Sammy started to clunk his way and I noticed she was still wearing Ryan's shoes.

"Can she at least get dressed first?" I asked.

Simmons looked uncertain. "Um—"

"Where's Mike? Where's Detective Stanton?" I demanded. I was not going to let Sammy plod around the police station in Ryan's way-too-big shoes and pants.

"What do you need, Fran?" Mike sounded weary.

"Can Sammy at least go get dressed before you haul her down to the station?"

He looked her up and down. "Yeah. Go." He sounded almost like he thought it was ridiculous that we even had to ask.

I looked at Simmons triumphantly as Sammy went inside to get dressed. He shrugged and didn't seem bothered which annoyed me. I crossed my arms over my chest as we waited in silence for Sammy to come back. When she finally did, I gave her a hug. "Call me when you're done, okay? I'm sure it won't be long." I stared pointedly at Mike, but he avoided looking back at me.

"You ready, Sammy?"

She nodded.

"Okay, let's go," he said and led her towards his car.

I watched them go, worried and wondering if I should have told her to call a lawyer after all.

Chapter 5

I PACED AROUND MY HOUSE, Latte tailing behind for what felt like hours. In fact, it was hours. And with every minute that went buy, my worry increased.

"Should I have told her to call a lawyer?" I asked as I paced by Matt.

"I feel like Mike would have told you if you needed to," he replied when I circled back to the living room.

Living room, kitchen, living room, foyer. Living room, kitchen, living room, foyer. It wasn't a very big circle, but at least it let Matt and I carry on something of a conversation. Not that there was much to it. It pretty much circled around the questions of whether I should have told her to call a lawyer, why they were keeping her so long, how could they think she or Ryan had anything to do with Cheryl's death.

Matt had an easy answer for that one. "They're just doing their jobs."

"But I'm the one who found the body and they didn't take me down to the station for an 'official statement.'"

"Yeah, but you didn't spend the night sleeping with a body in your backyard."

I stopped and stared at him. Saying it that way did make them seem more suspect, but still. "How do they know I didn't walk up and see Cheryl in the yard and kill her then?"

Matt raised his eyebrows. "Did you?"

"Well, no, but——"

"I'm sure they know that."

"But they have to know Ryan and Sammy didn't kill her either!"

Matt shrugged.

"Aargh!" I screamed out in frustration and resumed my pacing. Latte didn't, choosing instead to hop up on the couch to cuddle with Matt.

"Did you notice if Mike touched the body?" Matt asked a couple of laps later.

He had to wait until I got back from circling the kitchen. "I don't know. I think so. Maybe. Ryan definitely did. He took her pulse before he called the police."

A lap later, he got to make his point. "It's pretty cold out there. They could probably tell by her body temperature that you hadn't just killed her."

It made sense. But since it didn't make the case for Sammy's innocence, I wasn't a fan. "I could have snuck over and killed her during the night and then come back early this morning to 'find' her."

Matt raised an eyebrow. "Why are you trying so hard to make yourself look guilty?" he asked softly.

I stopped. "I'm not. I'm trying to make the case that if Sammy's a suspect, I may as well be one too."

"Did Mike take her away in handcuffs?"

"No."

"What about Ryan?"

I shook my head.

"There you go. They're not suspects."

I wasn't convinced and said so.

"Look." Matt stood up to Latte's dismay and came over to put his hands on my shoulders. He looked into my eyes. "Mike's a smart guy, right?"

I nodded.

"Ryan's a cop. Do you really think that if Ryan killed Cheryl, he would have just left the body in his own backyard?"

It did sound pretty ridiculous.

"And do you think that if Sammy killed her, she would have just left her there?"

I couldn't imagine Sammy killing someone in the first place, not to mention leaving the body out in the open like that. Forget leaving evidence, she would have felt bad leaving the body exposed. She got upset when she saw a dead possum on the street, and I was pretty sure she'd probably buried snuck off to bury one a time or two. Me, I didn't want to go near a possum under any circumstances, dead or alive.

"There you go. Even you can see that it doesn't make sense for Sammy or Ryan to have done it, and you're not a cop. I'm sure Mike and his guys just took them down as a formality."

"But then why is it taking so long?" I asked, and we were back to the beginning. Matt gave up and sat back down on the couch, which made Latte happy. I resumed my pacing. Fortunately, it didn't last long because my phone rang.

"Maybe it's Sammy!" I lunged to grab it off the end table. I looked at the caller ID. "It is!" I punched the button to answer it. "Sammy! Hi. Are you okay? Did they let you go? You're okay, aren't you?"

A sniffle.

"Sammy?"

"I'm okay," she said, though I could hear her voice wavering. "But—are you at home? Can I come talk to you?"

"Yes! Of course. Come on over. I'll be here. Do you need a ride?"

"No, I'll walk. I could use the fresh air."

We said our goodbyes and hung up. "Sammy's coming over."

"See? I told you they'd let her go."

"She sounded awful, like she's been crying."

Matt's response was a grunt. "Mm. Do you want me to stay while you talk to her?"

"Yes. No. No." I debated back and forth, finally deciding that Sammy might be more open with me without Matt around.

"You want me to go?"

"Yes."

"You two will be okay here alone? You're not going to do anything crazy like run off and try to solve the murder all by yourselves?"

"I have no intention of doing that."

Matt looked at me skeptically. I'd had no intention of getting involved with murder cases before, but I'd always ended up doing it anyway. And those cases hadn't even been ones where I found the body. Or where one of my best friends and employees was a suspect. I decided to hedge. "I promise I won't run off and solve the murder without telling you first."

Matt sighed. "That's probably the best I'm going to get, so I'll take it."

"You're a smart man." I smiled.

"Sometimes I'm not so sure." He kissed me and headed out the back door.

I flitted around the house, straightening up things I'd already straightened up, and getting some light refreshments ready. I knew it wasn't a social call, but I also knew that a round of cookies and eggnog could solve a lot of problems just on its own. At least, it had always helped me feel better when my mom served it to me after a rough day as a kid.

When I had everything ready and Sammy hadn't arrived yet, I started over, fiddling with pillows, picking imaginary lint off the couch, adjusting the cookies on the plate *just so*. I checked my phone to see if she'd called or left a message that I hadn't noticed. It seemed like she was taking a long time. I started to wonder if maybe they'd pulled her back into the police station just as she left. What if they'd arrested her?

I had just pulled up Mike's phone number when there was a knock on the door.

"Oh, thank God!" I flung my phone down on the couch and ran to open it.

Sammy looked as bad as she'd sounded on the phone. Maybe worse. Her nose and eyes were red, her blonde hair was falling out of the ponytail she'd hastily and sloppily pulled it into.

I grabbed her and hugged her. "Are you okay? What happened? Tell me everything."

I escorted her in and over to the couch where she slumped down without taking off her coat. I put a couple cookies on a plate and poured some eggnog into a cup and pushed them in front of her, then sat down next to her.

Sammy stared for a while before drawing a ragged breath. "I'm scared, Fran."

I took her hand and held it. "What happened?"

"They think I killed her."

Until now, I'd been able to tell myself that I was reading into things that weren't there, that they had probably taken Ryan and Sammy in because they had more questions to ask them—what time they'd gotten back to Ryan's house, did they hear any strange noises, stuff like that. But now—I wanted to comfort her.

"Did they actually say that or do you just think that's what they think?"

"Mike didn't say it, but he didn't have to. I could tell. He wasn't acting like himself. He wasn't friendly or smiling. He seemed like he was mad at me."

"That's probably just how he is when he's questioning someone."

She looked straight at me. "Was he like that with you?"

I hated to do it, but I shook my head.

Sammy sank further into the couch. "I've never been questioned by the police like that before. It was so scary. And it was like everything I said came out wrong. I told him about her following me to work and the texts she was sending me, but I could tell it just made him think that I had a reason to kill her." She looked over at me again. "You know I didn't kill her, don't you Fran?"

"Of course. Of course I do. You're the most gentle person I know."

She nodded sadly and went back to staring into space.

"Do you think it's possible that you just misinterpreted Mike's questions? Maybe he was trying to prove that you didn't do it, not that you did."

She shook her head against the couch, messing up her ponytail even more. "I don't think so. He kept twisting everything around to make it sound like it was a reason that I *did* kill her, not that I didn't. Have you ever had a boyfriend that turns all your words around to make it seem like everything's your fault?"

I nodded. Yup, I knew that type.

"It was like that. It just seemed like everything I said was wrong and meant that I killed her."

I tried to think of something helpful to say in response, but I couldn't.

"What about Ryan?" I asked after a few minutes of silence. I didn't really want to ask, partly because I knew that her boyfriend being the prime suspect instead of her wouldn't exactly be of much comfort, but if Sammy thought everything she told Mike had pointed to her as a suspect, wouldn't it also have pointed to Ryan? Didn't all the evidence that pointed to Sammy point just as much to Ryan?

Her shoulder twitched. "I don't know. I haven't talked to him. I tried to call, but—I guess he's still at the police station."

"Did Mike say anything about him?"

"That was another thing that came out all wrong.

I told him that Ryan knew about her coming to the café, but not about the texts, and as soon as I said it, he got this look on his face and I knew I was in even more trouble than before."

As soon as she said it out loud, I realized she was right. All along, she thought she was protecting Ryan from knowing what Cheryl was up to, but it ended up coming back to bite her. If Ryan didn't know about Cheryl harassing Sammy, he had no motive to kill her. I leaned back on the couch, too.

"Fran?" Sammy asked a few minutes later.

"Yeah?"

"You know I don't like to ask for favors, but——"

I interrupted her. "Of course I'll help you figure out who killed Cheryl. There's no way I'm letting you go to jail." I smiled at her and picked up one of the cookies on the table. "Besides, if you did, who would decorate all the cookies for the café?"

Chapter 6

I WAS ALONE in the café the next afternoon. I'd sent Sammy home early to get some rest after she admitted that, between worrying about being arrested and having nightmares about what would happen if she did, she'd barely slept the night before. She looked it, too. And acted it.

The café had been slow—on January 2, everyone was either getting back into their routines or hiding out before they had to—but even so, I'd caught her forgetting orders and mixing up drinks a couple times. Her going home early would be the best thing for everyone involved.

It also made it easier to have a private conversation about her situation.

Mike came in for his regular mid-afternoon pick-me-up right on time as far as I was concerned. Sammy was gone and the café was completely empty.

The perfect circumstances for what I wanted to talk to him about. I caught a glimpse of him walking down the street on his way to the café, so I went ahead and prepared his large coffee to go—very strong, very black, just the way he liked it.

"Hey, Franny, how you doing?" he asked as he walked in the door, setting the little bell jingling. "Slow day today?"

He seemed like he was in a good mood, which was a relief. He'd been grumpier than usual the past few weeks, especially right before Christmas. It was a stressful time of year for everyone, but Mike had been another level of short-tempered. Granted, I'd been poking my nose in one of his cases, but I'd done that before and he hadn't completely lost his cool over it. Especially not multiple times. And he'd definitely never stopped coming to the café for days on end before. It had been bad. But he seemed like he was back to his old self again, and I was grateful. Especially because of what I was about to do.

"Yup, I think everyone gave up caffeine for the new year." I slid his coffee across the counter to him, but kept my hand on it.

"Maybe everyone else did, but I sure didn't," he said and grinned. He made a move to take his coffee cup, but I was still holding on to it. "Fran?"

"Do you have a minute?"

For a second I thought he was going to say no, just

based on the way he was looking at me, but then he sighed. "Sure, why not?"

I let go of his coffee cup. "Great! Pick a table and I'll be over as soon as I make myself a drink."

He sighed again as he picked up his coffee and went for the closest table. I had a feeling he was already reconsidering agreeing to talk to me, but I wasn't going to let that stop me.

I pulled a couple shots of espresso into a cup and topped it with barely enough milk to make it count as a cappuccino, then grabbed some cookies and headed over to the table. "Here, have some cookies," I said as I sat it down in the middle of the table.

Mike picked up a large snowflake-shaped sugar cookie topped with silvery white icing and an abundance of clear sprinkles. He studied it for a minute, then shrugged and took a big bite.

I took his chewing as a prime opportunity to start talking. "So, Sammy seemed pretty shaken up yesterday after talking to you." I could tell he immediately regretted sitting down, or maybe taking the bite of cookie that rendered him mute, but, either way, I wasn't going to let it stop me. "For some reason, she seems to think she's your prime suspect."

He raised his eyebrows and kept chewing. It was a big bite of cookie.

"But that can't be right, can it? I mean, you've known Sammy for years! You can't possibly think she would kill someone! You remember a couple of months ago when she thought there was a mouse in her apartment? She made the landlord put out no-kill traps because she couldn't stand the thought of the mouse dying when it was just trying to find a warm place to sleep! If a person won't kill a mouse, they can't possibly be capable of killing a person, can they?"

Mike held up a finger while he finished chewing and then sipped his coffee. I waited for him to tell me that Sammy's interview was just a formality and of course he knew she didn't kill Cheryl. Instead, he just said, "You'd be surprised."

I stared at him. "Mike. You can't possibly think that Sammy killed Cheryl."

"You know I can't discuss ongoing investigations."

"You can at least tell me if she's really your prime suspect, can't you?"

"I can't discuss ongoing investigations."

I glared sullenly at him and sipped my cappuccino. It was definitely heavy on the espresso, but at least it was good espresso. Mike took a bite of cookie and stared back at me. I couldn't read his expression, which was annoying at the moment, but I imagined was useful when he was interrogating people. They would have no idea what he was thinking with a face like that. I thought about poor Sammy facing that in the interrogation room when she was used to smiling, joking Mike who was just looking for his caffeine fix. No wonder she thought he was mad at her. But then I realized, "You don't thinks he did it, do you?"

"Fran—" There was a warning tone in his voice that I chose to ignore.

"You don't! Mike, you know she's terrified, don't you? She thinks you really believe she's a murderer."

"Fran—" There was that tone again, but I wasn't planning to pay attention to it now.

"You need to let her know that you're not just waiting around for the right moment to arrest her. I sent her home today because she didn't get any sleep last night. She's worrying herself sick!"

A glimmer of something like remorse flickered across his face, but he was back to the stony-faced investigator a fraction of a second later. His jaw flexed. I waited. He looked around the café like he was hoping someone would appear to save him from the conversation, but we were alone and there wasn't even any foot traffic out on the sidewalk to give him hope that someone might pop in. January was the absolute low time for tourist traffic in our little beach town.

Finally, he turned to look at me. "I have to go where the evidence leads me."

"And it's leading you to Sammy?"

"Right now, yes."

"But what about Ryan? The body was in *his* backyard."

"Ryan didn't have a motive."

"Yes he did."

Mike cocked an eyebrow.

"To get her to stop harassing Sammy."

Mike sighed. "Ryan didn't know about what Cheryl had been doing recently. As far as he knew, everything stopped when you kicked Cheryl out of the café."

"*As far as you know.*"

"Trust me, Fran. He didn't know until I showed them to him. I've been doing this long enough now to know when people are lying, and he wasn't lying."

I silently wished I'd pushed Sammy harder to tell Ryan about the texts. Or that I'd told him myself. Or told Mike. Or anybody really. "So she's your prime suspect."

"Unfortunately, yes."

I clasped my cappuccino cup with both hands and stared down into it. "She didn't do it, Mike," I said after a moment.

He waited even longer before he replied. "I know. But I can't let my personal feelings get in the way of objectivity. Not when the evidence we have so far points to her. Not until I have evidence that leads me somewhere else."

"And you think you'll find it? Before—before it's too late?"

"I'm trying, Franny. I'm really trying." He stood up to go.

"What can I do to help?" I asked.

"Stay out of it. I mean it. Don't get involved. Just let me handle it."

I nodded reluctantly. I didn't know if that was a promise I would keep, but I had faith in Mike and knew he wouldn't rush to arrest Sammy if there was anything he could do to help it.

I gave Mike a fresh cup of coffee to replace the one he'd drained—seriously, the man may as well have just set up an IV drip of it—and popped the rest of the cookies into a bag. The café was still empty and I was glad because my mind was on Sammy, and I didn't know if I could refocus it on customers very quickly.

Mike was almost out the door when he stopped and turned around. "There is one thing you can do for Sammy," he said.

I looked up eagerly, hoping he was going to tell me about some piece of evidence he needed that he couldn't get on his own. That wasn't it.

"Tell her to get a lawyer."

Chapter 7

AFTER I CLOSED up the café for the night, I went to see Sammy at Ryan's house. She said she didn't want to be home alone in her apartment, and I couldn't really blame her. After saying hello, Ryan made an excuse about wanting to watch a football game and disappeared to his bedroom, leaving me and Sammy alone in the living room.

"How're you holding up?" I asked. "Did you manage to get any sleep this afternoon?"

"Not really."

"Well, maybe tonight."

"Maybe." She was curled up in an armchair, staring at her lap. She'd looked happy enough to see me when I came in, but now any energy she'd had seemed to have drained out of her. I wasn't sure if it was the stress, or the lack of sleep, or both.

"I talked to Mike today."

A glimmer of hope flitted across her face. "Any good news?"

I thought about fudging the truth and telling her that Mike believed that she was innocent, but I didn't want to lie to her, even if it was technically not really a lie. "Well, you know how Mike is. Doesn't want to talk the case, wants me to stay out of it, blah blah blah." I'd hoped it would make her laugh, but all I got was a twitch of her lips that I could almost pretend was a smile. "He, um, he said, uh," I tried to think of a way to cushion the message he'd told me to give her, but I didn't know that it was possible. I also sort of hoped that if I stalled long enough, it would give Mike a chance to burst through the door to declare that he'd caught the real killer. I had no reason to think that might happen, but I still half-hoped it would.

Sammy looked at me expectantly, waiting for me to tell her whatever it was that Mike had said. I bit the bullet. "He said to tell you to get a lawyer."

Sammy's eyes got big, and then she squeezed them closed tight. She took a deep, slow, shaky breath and sat there for a long time before she opened her eyes again. "Do you know any good ones?"

"Just the one."

"Giorgio DiGiorgio it is then."

It almost went without saying. Giorgio DiGiorgio, ridiculous name and all, was *the* guy when it came to lawyers in Cape Bay and the surrounding towns. He was as well-known as a shady TV lawyer except without being on TV or, as far as I knew, being shady. He handled all sorts of cases for all sorts of people and did it well apparently. I'd even heard that he'd somehow represented both sides in a divorce recently and both people walked away happy, saying they wouldn't hesitate to hire him again. It was strange, but so were lots of things when you lived in a small town.

Sammy took a deep breath. "I'll call him in the morning."

I nodded, wishing I had something to say to make her feel better. I didn't. "I'm sure he'll know how to help you."

She nodded. If it was possible, she looked even more dejected than before. Not that I could say I'd feel any different in her shoes. Going knowing you're a suspect to the police officer investigating you suggesting you should get a lawyer had to be rough. It made it more real somehow. I know it felt a lot more real to me and I wasn't even the one looking at a murder trial. I shivered. Just thinking those words —"murder trial"—sent a chill down my spine. No wonder Sammy was so freaked out.

I stayed with Sammy a while longer, trying to chat and cheer her up and take her mind off things, but I knew it wasn't helping. I finally gave her a hug and said goodbye, hoping that she'd be able to get some rest. She was going to need it.

I slept fitfully that night. I kept having nightmares

about Sammy being dragged away by the police, or me coming into the café only to find it unattended because Sammy had been arrested. I finally got up and made myself a cup of coffee to drink while I sat on the couch watching infomercials with Latte. That's where I was when Sammy called me at nine-fifteen. The infomercial pickings had gotten slim by that time, but I wasn't up for the morning news talk shows.

"Is everything okay?" I asked her.

"I'm really sorry for the short notice, but I called Giorgio DiGiorgio's office, and I have an appointment at ten."

It was so like Sammy to apologize for not giving me more notice that she had a last-minute meeting with the lawyer I'd told her she needed to talk to. "Don't worry about it! I'll come in to take care of the café. I can be there in fifteen minutes."

"Actually, I was wondering if you could come with me."

"Oh, do you need a ride?" I knew Sammy had a car, but maybe it was broken down. This time of year was rough on vehicles. It wasn't ideal to shut the café down for a couple of hours in the middle of the day, but I wasn't going to reject Sammy if she needed me.

"No. I want you to come talk to him with me."

"For moral support? Wouldn't you rather have Ryan? Or Dawn?"

I heard her take a deep breath through the phone. For a second, I thought she was going to agree, but she didn't. "No, not for moral support. I mean, yes, but—" Another deep breath. "If you're going to help me, wouldn't it be good for you to hear what he says?"

I thought for a moment. I probably didn't need to hear what Giorgio DiGiorgio said to help me solve the case, but it couldn't hurt. It would at least help me know what he thought about the police's case against Sammy. Besides, she didn't deny that she wanted the moral support. "Of course. Of course I'll come. I can be ready in fifteen minutes. Do you want to pick me up?"

"Can you drive? The heat in my car is on the fritz again."

"Sure thing," I said and told her goodbye. "Sorry, Latte," I told him, jostling him off my lap. He looked sad that his pillow was leaving. I scratched him under the chin. "I'll take you for a nice, long walk when I get back. I promise." He laid his head down on his paws and looked up at me with his very best puppy dog eyes. I momentarily wondered if I could just bring him with us, but almost immediately decided it was a bad idea. He'd have to stay in the car and I didn't want him to get cold. I patted him on the head. "Sorry. I'd take you if I could."

Fifteen minutes later, I was dressed and ready to go. I promised Latte one more time that we'd go for a long walk when I got back and headed to pick up Sammy. I pulled up on the street in front of the café and she came right out, locking the door behind her. I felt a little pang seeing the café closed up in the middle of the day—well, the morning anyway—but I took solace in the fact that I was doing something kind for a friend.

"Thanks for coming with me," she said as she got settled in her seat. "I really appreciate it."

"No problem." I eased the car back out onto the road and turned it to head towards the lawyer's office in the next town over.

"I called Rhonda. She was getting her hair done, but she said she'd come over to the café as soon as she was done so it won't be closed the whole time we're gone."

I smiled gratefully. Here she was, on her way to talk to a lawyer about a murder case, and she took the time to think about the café. That was why she was my second-in-command.

Sammy pulled up the directions on her phone, and between her and the computerized female voice that pronounced every other street name wrong, it wasn't long before we pulled up in front of the lawyer's office, nestled in a long, low brick building in an office park and flanked by a dry cleaner's on one side and a uniform supply company on the other. The name was emblazoned above his doors. "The Law Offices of Giorgio DiGiorgio & Associates." I wasn't aware of any associates, but I'd never actually been there, or even seen DiGiorgio in person, so maybe they were in there somewhere and just didn't get any of the press.

I looked over at Sammy as she stared up at the sign. She looked more than a little overwhelmed. "You ready?" I asked her.

She took a deep breath, then nodded. "Ready as I'll ever be."

Before she could change her mind, we got out and headed for our appointment with Giorgio DiGiorgio.

Chapter 8

STEPPING into Giorgio DiGiorgio's offices felt like stepping into a different world. The reception area was bare except for a very large, very ornate mahogany desk that was of a style that made it look like it been built before my grandparents came to America. The floor was covered in a thick, plush, dark green carpet that looked more like something you'd see in a very rich person's house than in a borderline run-down office park, and the dark wood-paneled walls had large paintings that I suspected had cost a pretty penny. One even looked like it was by Louis Cliffton, an artist I'd recently had the privilege to meet. A crystal chandelier hung from the ceiling. Someone had either spent a lot of money decorating the place or a lot of time making it look like they had.

"Wow," Sammy whispered beside me. "It's nothing at all like I pictured."

"You know, I think it's exactly what I pictured. I never thought it would actually look like this, but when I think of Giorgio DiGiorgio, this is pretty much what I imagine."

"I think you're right." Sammy nodded.

An impeccably-groomed woman appeared from the back with a practiced smile. "Samantha Ericksen?" I wondered if this was one of the "associates" from the sign above the door.

"That's me." Sammy stepped forward. "But you can call me Sammy."

The woman made a note on the clipboard she carried. "Will your friend be joining us?"

"Yes." Sammy nodded, then hesitated. "Is that okay?"

"Of course. Your name?"

"Francesca Amaro. Fran."

The woman nodded and made a note on her clipboard. "Follow me, please." The woman led us down a long hallway, lined with heavy-looking wood doors that matched the paneling. I self-consciously clutched my handbag against my body—the jingling of my keys inside it was surprisingly loud in the quiet environment. Our footsteps didn't even make noise as we walked. I wondered if that was the point of the thick carpeting—to keep things quiet.

Almost at the end of the hallway, the woman opened a door. "You can wait here. Mr. DiGiorgio will be with you shortly."

Sammy and I walked into the room. It was a waiting room. The walls were lined with chairs, a TV on muted cable news hung on the wall, and there were piles of magazines on the end tables.

"This is a weird place for a waiting room," I said, sitting down in an amazingly comfortable chair and picking up a magazine. It struck me as strange that it was one of those celebrity tabloids you see in the checkout line at the supermarket. I held it up to Sammy. "I would have expected something classier."

"Celebrity divorce scandals aren't classy?" The first genuine smile I'd seen on Sammy's face for days spread across her face.

I looked at the magazine cover. "These two? No." I picked up another issue of the same magazine from the pile. "Now these two, maybe."

"Ooh! Let me look at that one. I love those two!" I handed her the magazine and picked the less-classy couple issue up off my lap.

Sammy caught my eye and smiled.

I shrugged. "I didn't say I wanted classy."

I was about halfway through the magazine when the same woman opened the door again, so it was probably about five minutes later—those magazines do not take long to read, if reading is even what you can call it. "Mr. DiGiorgio is ready for you now. Follow me, please."

Putting the magazine aside somewhat reluctantly (I did, after all, want to know the shocking details the celebrity couple's nanny was going to spill), I followed Sammy and the woman back into the hallway. We walked to the end of the hall where the woman knocked on a door.

"Come in!" The voice that answered was booming even through the door.

The woman opened the door and ushered us in. "Mr. DiGiorgio, this is Samantha Ericksen, your client. She is accompanied by Francesca Amaro. They go by Sammy and Fran."

I felt a bit like I was being introduced at a debutant ball as we stepped into the room that was somehow even more lavishly decorated than the rest of the office was. His big desk was a larger, more ornate version of the one in the reception area. There was a wet bar in the corner stocked with as many bottles of liquor as you'd find at a well-stocked restaurant and bookshelves lined the rest of the walls, full of hundreds—thousands?—of leather-bound books. While it looked the same, the carpet was somehow even more plush, so much so that my feet actually sank into it.

"Wonderful to meet you!" Giorgio DiGiorgio boomed. He was not the kind of man you could miss. I'd seen pictures of him in the paper, but they didn't do justice to the man in real life. He was tall and broad-shouldered and looked like he worked out—not too much, but just enough to define his physique. He had silver-and-black hair that was so perfectly salt-

and-peppered that I couldn't help but wonder if he had some help getting it that way. Under that thick, lustrous hair, he had brilliant blue eyes that seemed to glow and, again, I wondered if they had help achieving that color. I didn't wonder about his skin though. A tan of that degree wasn't easy to come by naturally in the summer in Massachusetts, let alone the winter.

His clothes, of course, fit the bigger-than-life image. Along with a blue shirt that rivaled his eyes in its brightness, he wore a tie that was almost hot pink, and a gray pinstripe suit, obviously precisely tailored, and made out of a material that had to cost a fortune —it had a subtle sheen, not a shine like some really cheap suits, but more like it was specially lit. I looked up to make sure it wasn't and almost choked when I noticed the light fixture—I'd been so busy looking at everything else that I'd somehow missed the massive —*massive*—crystal chandelier on the ceiling. Compared to this one, the one in the lobby looked tiny.

"Sammy!" He engulfed Sammy's hand in his and shook it. "Fran!" He repeated the same thing with mine. "Can I get you anything? Some water, perhaps? Georgia, get Sammy and Fran some water, would you, please? And some cookies? Some cookies, too, please, Georgia. They're from a bakery just down the street. They're wonderful, you'll love them!" He flashed us a brilliant, gleamingly white grin. I was also pretty sure it was safe to assume that was not natural, since I had never seen teeth that seemed to glow on their own before. I wondered if he got juries to acquit his clients just by dazzling and overwhelming. Charming them, too. The man oozed charm and somehow, that, of all things, actually felt genuine.

"Have a seat ladies!"

We sat and, as soon as we did, I wondered if I would ever get up again. If I thought the chair in the waiting room was incredibly comfortable, it was nothing compared to the ones in Giorgio DiGiorgio's office. I sank down into it, content to stay as long as I could. It was by far the most comfortable chair I'd ever had the pleasure of sitting in.

Georgia brought over three glasses of water and a platter of cookies. I restrained myself from immediately reaching out and grabbing one. Well, until Giorgio DiGiorgio did and declared that we should, "Eat! Eat, please, ladies! If you don't, then I'll eat them, and I won't be able to fit into my suit." He leaned forward and winked at us. "It's custom, you know."

I knew. Strictly out of politeness, I took one of the cookies broke off a piece, and put it in my mouth. It was good. Very good. I couldn't help but think that it wasn't quite as good as the ones I made and sold in the café, but I wasn't going to say that.

After we'd finished our cookies, Giorgio DiGiorgio sat back in his chair and nodded over at Georgia, who

I realized had taken a seat behind a small desk off to the side. "So, let's get down to business. My assistant Georgia will be taking notes, if you don't mind. So Sammy, tell me what's going on."

Sammy slowly began to describe the situation with me jumping in here and there to remind her of details she'd missed or to give my own perspective. She told him about Cheryl's harassment at the café, the creepy text messages she'd sent, me finding Cheryl's body in Ryan's yard—here he gave me a meaningful look and then looked back over his shoulder at Georgia who met his gaze and nodded. Sammy continued, telling him about the interrogation. She gave him details she hadn't mentioned to me that made me squirm in my seat. From the sound of it, Mike really had been pretty hard on her. No wonder she was worried. She finished the story by telling him that Mike had suggested she get a lawyer.

Giorgio DiGiorgio sat still in his chair, his elbows rested on the arms of the chair with his fingers tented in front of him the whole time she spoke. The only reaction he gave was when she mentioned that I was the one who found the body. After she was done, he kept sitting there, occasionally drumming his tented fingers against each other. We sat in silence for what felt like a long time, so long that I began to wonder if it was a tactic of his—make the potential client uncomfortable enough that she starts to blab things she hadn't meant to. Or maybe make the client's friend uncomfortable enough to blurt something out. But I knew Sammy had told him everything and I had nothing to blurt out, so we just sat there in silence while we waited for Giorgio DiGiorgio to say something.

"Now Sammy," he began, finally breaking the silence. "If I take your case, and that's an *if*, you have to commit to telling me the truth about everything, one hundred percent of the time, no matter how uncomfortable that truth may make you. Any question I ask you, you need to be completely honest with me, do you understand? Completely honest."

If Giorgio DiGiorgio knew anything about her, he wouldn't have had to ask. Sammy nodded solemnly.

"If I take your case, I will ask you a lot of questions. Some things you may not be comfortable with. They will seem rude, intrusive even. But I will need your honest answers, no matter what the question, so that I can defend you properly. Does that make sense?"

Sammy nodded again. "Yes, it does."

"Now there is one thing I will never ask you and under no circumstances do I want you to volunteer this information to me." He paused and looked her dead in the eye. "I will *never* ask you if you killed that woman."

"But I didn't!" Sammy blurted out.

Giorgio DiGiorgio held up a finger and smiled.

"Ah-ah-ah, what did I just say? That's the one thing we're *not* going to talk about."

"But I didn't kill her!"

Before Giorgio DiGiorgio could reprimand her again, I stepped in. "*Why*, Mr. DiGiorgio? Can you tell us *why* you don't want her to tell you that?"

Giorgio DiGiorgio smiled at me. "Because as soon as she does, I can't truthfully say to the court that you didn't do it."

"But I didn't!" Sammy's voice came out as nearly a shriek.

Now Giorgio DiGiorgio smiled at her. "Well, if you're going to tell me, that's the right thing to tell me. Say you're innocent all you want, but don't ever tell me you're guilty."

"I won't because I'm not!"

"That's good, that's good. Now let me give you the one exception to that rule. The one exception is if we decide on a self-defense plea. If we decide on a self-defense plea, I need you to tell me everything, and I do mean everything. You cannot leave one detail out. If you do, and the prosecution knows that detail, they can use it to destroy us. Along those lines, if we decide to plead guilty, then I also need to know everything. You can't assume there's anything the prosecution won't find out, and I can't be surprised by anything. Now do you understand that exception?"

It seemed to me more like two exceptions than one, and both of them seemed to cancel out his saying that he would "never" ask her if she did it, but it didn't seem like the place or time to bring either of those things up.

"Yes, I understand it," Sammy said. "But I didn't kill her, so it won't matter."

"Good, good. Georgia?"

As if expecting to be beckoned over at any second, Georgia rose and walked over to Giorgio DiGiorgio.

"The paper Georgia's about to give you has on it my hourly fee and the retainer I will need up front before I can begin working on your case." He looked at Georgia and nodded. She handed the paper to Sammy who opened it up and coughed. I leaned over and she turned it towards me. Both numbers made my eyes water. "Will that be acceptable?"

Sammy glanced at me. I raised my shoulders in an I-can't-answer-that shrug. Calling it a big chunk of change was an understatement. Calling it an understatement was an understatement. But I didn't know any other lawyers in the area, and I didn't think she'd be able to find any cheaper in Boston. Besides, from the way Mike was talking, she didn't have time to shop around.

"Okay," Sammy said finally.

"Excellent. Georgia will draw up the paperwork." Georgia retreated to her desk and resumed tapping on her computer. "This consultation is, of course, complimentary." He picked up the cookie plate. "Another cookie anyone? More water?"

Sammy and I both shook our heads. I wasn't sure either of us would be up for cookies any time soon.

"Let's get to it, then. I have to admit, Sammy, from what you've described, it doesn't look good for you. It's still early, of course, so there's plenty of time for the police to find evidence implicating someone else, but the fact that they seem so set on you and, let's be honest, told you to get a lawyer, isn't a good sign. They may have more information that points to you that we don't know about yet."

"Like what?" I asked, leaning forward.

He turned his palms upward. "There could be physical evidence, something on the body that points to you. There could have been something on her cell phone that points to you. Someone may have seen you with her—"

"I wasn't with her," Sammy said quickly.

"Maybe someone thought they saw you with her. Eyewitness testimony is notoriously unreliable, but it can be very convincing. And it can be all the police need to be encouraged to look in a certain direction."

"Are you suggesting that someone is setting Sammy up?" I asked.

"Do you have reason to believe someone might do that?"

I looked at Sammy. She shook her head.

"Then no. It's something to be aware of, but it's entirely possible that it's a case of mistaken identity. And, of course, this is entirely conjecture. It could be any number of things drawing their attention in your direction. There's no way for us to know at this point. Now, in light of that fact, it's difficult for me to formulate a defense. With the facts I have at this point, a self-defense plea would be a longshot—"

"But I didn't do it."

Giorgio DiGiorgio nodded and held up a finger. "I understand that, but the fact of the matter is that we have to explore all avenues, and a preliminary exploration of the self-defense avenue looks like a dead end. The fact that you deny seeing the victim—"

"Because I didn't."

"—along with the fact that she, according to you, never actually physically threatened you, and the fact you never reported the harassment to the police, mean we'll have to go in a different direction. Unless you have more information you want to share with me?"

Sammy shook her head vehemently.

"Well, then, self-defense is out. But, that's fine. We'll have plenty of time for that to explore defense strategies. Right now, what we have to focus on is keeping you out of jail as long as possible and, if you end up there, getting you out as quickly as possible."

Sammy swallowed hard and I reached out to squeeze her hand.

"First of all, I understand you consider yourself friendly with this detective, but under no circumstances should you speak to him without me being present. Should you be arrested or asked to come back in for questioning, you need to call me, from the station if necessary. Let them know you're invoking your right to counsel, and then do not say another word until I arrive." Giorgio DiGiorgio waited until Sammy nodded her agreement, then continued. "And in case we're not clear, let me remind you what's on the line. A murder conviction. If you're charged with and convicted of this crime, you could easily spend the rest of your life in prison. That's not a place a girl like you wants to be."

I was pretty sure that was something Sammy didn't need to be told, but it brought it home all the same.

Giorgio DiGiorgio relaxed back in his chair, letting his hands rest on the arms of his chair. "Now do you have any questions for me?"

Sammy looked over at me. I tried to think of something, but I couldn't. My brain was swirling too much with everything he'd said so far. Sammy shook her head. "No," she said, her voice coming out hoarse and scratchy.

"That's totally understandable. It's a lot to take in all at once. Please feel free to call me if you do think of anything." He smiled. "That will, of course, be billed at my hourly rate."

Sammy visibly flinched.

"Well, if that's all, Georgia will help you get all the paperwork signed and the finances taken care of and then will see you out. Thank you both for coming in." Giorgio DiGiorgio stood up, shook both our hands, and circled around to sit down behind his desk.

Georgia came over and escorted us back out to the lobby where she had Sammy sign a sheaf of papers before asking how she'd like to pay the exorbitant retainer fee. "We take cash, checks, and credit, although there is, of course, an additional fee if you pay that way."

"Of course," I muttered as Sammy dug in her purse for her wallet. I cringed for her as she pulled out a credit card and reluctantly handed it over to Georgia. I made a mental note that I needed find a way to help her raise some money to cover some of that fee.

Once Georgia had run the card and turned it back over to Sammy with a large packet of papers, including copies of everything she'd signed and some other things—I guessed notes from the meeting and, from the looks of it, a list of Giorgio DiGiorgio's do's and don'ts for his clients. With that done, we headed back out to the car.

We sat there for a minute, letting the engine warm up and staring into space as we both processed the last hour.

"Your cookies are better than the ones he had," Sammy said after a few minutes.

I smiled. "Thanks." I looked over at her. "I thought so too."

She started to giggle.

"And did you notice her name is Georgia? Giorgio DiGiorgio's assistant is named Georgia? How likely is that?"

"Maybe it's why he hired her," she laughed. "Maybe he only hires people with George in their names."

"Or they all have to change their names to George. It's a condition of employment."

A boisterous laugh burst from Sammy's lips. I was so happy to hear her sounding so happy, and her laugh made me laugh. I accidentally snorted, and she laughed harder. We sat in the car and laughed until we cried, and then kept going until I wasn't sure whether the tears were from laughter or sorrow.

Chapter 9

I CONVINCED Sammy to take the afternoon off and dropped her off at Ryan's so she could talk to him about everything Giorgio DiGiorgio had said. When I got to the café, Rhonda was behind the counter, reading a book.

"Things a little slow?" I asked.

"We've had a couple people come by." She closed the book and flipped it over, but not before I caught sight of a shirtless hunk on its cover. Somehow, I wasn't surprised. "I cleaned the coffee machines, reorganized the cold display case, and ground some beans, but after an hour or so, I figured I may as well get some reading in."

"Fine by me," I said and headed to the espresso machine to make myself a drink. "Do we still have any of that eggnog?"

"I think there's some in the back. You want me to get it?"

"Please." I began pulling the espresso shots for my drink. Shots, plural. I was in the mood for plenty of caffeine. I inhaled deeply to take in as much of the coffee's aroma as I could. It smelled so good.

Rhonda put the pitcher of eggnog down on the counter and eyed me as I poured some into a stainless steel pitcher and began to steam it. "Whatcha makin'?"

"Eggnog latte. Want one?"

She hesitated for a second, then shrugged. "Sure, why not? You're probably not trying to poison me."

I grinned. "Probably not."

With the eggnog steamed and ready, I lifted the pitcher to pour it into the espresso but paused. Every cup of coffee I made at the café, I poured the milk so that its white color created a design against the darker brown crema of the espresso. I don't like to brag, but I could make some pretty sophisticated pictures, either pouring freehand or using a toothpick or one of the little brushes I kept for the purpose to create fine details. Sometimes I even used a little bit of chocolate syrup, cinnamon, or sugar to really do it up. But eggnog was much thicker than milk and I wasn't sure if I could create the same effects with it that I could with regular milk. But there was no better drink to try it on than my own.

I poured slowly and carefully, and managed to

create a passable rosetta. Not my best work, but not bad for eggnog.

I made Rhonda's drink, pulling off a slightly better rosetta, and passed it to her. She looked skeptical as she sniffed it. "I dunno."

"Oh, just try it! It's good."

"Espresso and eggnog? Really?"

"Just drink it."

"You first."

I rolled my eyes, but took a sip of the latte. It was good. Excellent, even.

"Well?"

"It's good. I knew that before I made you one."

She hesitated, but eventually raised it to her lips. It took a long time before she actually sipped it though. When she did, she smiled. "That's really good!"

"I told you it was!"

She shrugged. "You could have been lying. It's too bad it's the end of eggnog season. We could have put this on the menu."

"I know, we'll have to remember it for next year."

We both sipped our lattes for a few minutes before Rhonda spoke again. "So how was the meeting with the lawyer?"

I made a face.

"That bad, huh?"

"We just have to figure out who really killed Cheryl."

"You make it sound so easy."

"It's not, but I don't have a choice. I can't just cross my fingers and hope the police move on from Sammy. I have to do everything I can to help her."

"Mike can't possibly think she actually did it."

"He doesn't, but—" I shrugged my shoulders.

"But he can't do anything if he doesn't have the evidence," she finished for me.

I nodded and we both went back to silently sipping our coffee, though now our minds were on Sammy.

"Speak of the devil," Rhonda said a few minutes later, nodding at the door behind me."

I turned to see Mike coming in. "Hey Mike!"

"It's been slow today, so I'll make you a fresh pot of coffee," Rhonda said, setting her cup down and heading for the regular machine.

"Thanks," he said. He looked tense.

"Everything going okay?" I asked.

He hesitated, then nodded.

"Any news about Sammy's case?""

His jaw clenched. "Back there," he said, pointing towards the back room that doubled as a storage room and office.

I gestured for him to lead the way and followed him, my mind racing. Why did he want to talk to me in private? It was just Rhonda out there, after all. I caught Rhonda's eye as I walked past her and knew she was wondering the same thing. Was it good news or bad news? If it was good news, he wouldn't have any reason not to say it in front of Rhonda, would he? Unless maybe it wasn't ready to be public yet. But he'd had to know I'd tell her right away. Unless he just didn't want to be the one spreading the news, even if he knew it would get out anyway.

I shut the door behind us. "What's up?"

His jaw clenched.

I waited.

"I'm off Sammy's case."

"You found another suspect?" I asked, feeling the excitement well up inside me.

If it was possible, his face muscles tightened even more. "No. But it's not my case anymore."

I finally realized what he was saying. "What? Why? Who's taking over? Is it because you and Sammy are friends?"

He did that jaw clenching thing again. "No, it's at least partly because, according to the Chief, I can't seem to solve any cases on my own."

A wave of guilt washed over me. I was the one getting involved in his cases and making it so he wasn't solving his cases on his own.

"But it's mainly because of what happened on the Underwood case."

I cringed. That one had gotten pretty out of hand. "But that wasn't your fault—"

"Chief doesn't care whose fault it was. He just wants me off the case."

I wanted to ask him if the Underwood case was

also why he had to work both Christmas Eve and New Year's Eve, but I didn't want to kick the man while he was down. "So who's taking over?" I knew it couldn't be Ryan and the Cape Bay Police Department was too small to have anyone else who really served in a detective role.

"He's bringing in someone from MSP."

"MSP?" I tried to figure out if that was a nearby town that he was getting someone on loan from, and then I realized with a gasp. "Massachusetts State Police?"

He nodded curtly.

"That's—that's not going to be good for Sammy, is it?"

He shook his head. "The biggest thing Sammy had going for her was that we all knew her and knew she's not a killer. Now though—" He turned his palms up in a hopeless gesture.

"That's not good," I murmured.

"There's more."

"There's more?" I sank down into a chair. "What is it?"

"We got the preliminary forensics in."

"And?"

He hesitated and took a breath. "I probably shouldn't tell you this, but—" He stopped and shrugged. "Based on the bruises around Cheryl's neck, the person who strangled her was petite. Small hands. Probably a woman."

I swallowed hard. That wasn't good.

"We weren't able to recover any fingerprints, but we did swab for DNA and—"

"No," I whispered.

"—there was a match to Sammy's DNA. Despite Sammy's claim that she didn't see Cheryl that night, the DNA evidence indicates that she touched her."

Time felt like it slowed down as I tried to process everything Mike had said. He was off the case. The murderer was probably a woman. Sammy's DNA was on Cheryl's body. I felt like I couldn't breathe, and I wasn't even the one who was a suspect. But why wasn't I?

"But I'm a woman. I have small hands." I stood and held them up to demonstrate. "I touched the body, so my DNA should be on it, too, right? Why aren't I a suspect then? Shouldn't I be just as much a suspect as Sammy?"

Mike's face darkened in an instant. "Dammit, Fran, stop being such a smartass! Stop acting like you're a cop. You're not. Leave the police work to the police for once. Just stay out of it. Do you think you can do that? Or do you want to end up with a gun to your head again? Or a rock bouncing off your skull? Or would you rather just accuse an innocent old man of a serious crime? You can't keep getting involved in things that aren't your business! I won't always be there to rescue you! I won't be there to save you this time, Fran! You need to lay off and *stay out of it*!"

At first I just stood there. And then I got mad. He'd been acting like this for weeks now—calm and rational one second, screaming and yelling the next. "What is *wrong* with you lately? One second, you're acting like a normal human being and the next you're a raving lunatic! You're being an abrasive jerk and if you keep it up, you're not going to be welcome here anymore! You can't just come in here and yell at me for asking a question. Seriously, what is your problem?"

Mike stared at me, his jaw clenched so tight the muscles bulged on the side of his face. I stared back. I was done with him and his attitude. Yes, he was my friend and, yes, it probably wasn't a good idea to upset the detective who was on Sammy's side, even if he wasn't officially on the case anymore, but I'd had enough. One minute, he was my old friend Mike and the next he was an angry stranger. I didn't like the angry stranger and, frankly, I didn't care if he never came back to my café.

I expected him to start yelling again, but he was still staring, his jaw working, clenching and unclenching. I wasn't going to wait anymore, not for him to start yelling at me. But before I could make a move to leave, his whole body deflated.

"Sandra asked me to move out."

"What?"

"Sandra asked me to move out," he said again, his voice hoarse.

"Oh, Mike!" I reached out and gave him a hug. "When? What happened? Sorry, nevermind, it's none of my business."

"Just before Christmas. And nothing happened, she just got tired of me working all the time. She said that if she was going to feel like a single mother, she may as well be one."

"Oh. Oh wow." I didn't know what to say. I didn't know if there even was anything to say. "I'm so sorry."

"Thanks." He poked at his eye and I realized he was fighting off tears.

I opened the door to the café and stuck my head out. "Is Mike's coffee ready yet?"

Rhonda handed it to me. "Is everything okay in there?" she asked quietly.

"Yeah, just—" I stopped. "Yeah." I shut the door again and handed Mike his coffee. "Here. Drink this. It'll make you feel better."

"Thanks." He tipped it back and took a long swallow of it. His throat had to be made of steel. That coffee was hot. "No whisky?" he asked me, a glint in his eye.

"Sorry, officer, you're on duty. Unless that's why got pulled off the case. You haven't been drinking on the job, have you?"

He made a noise that sounded like he was trying to laugh, but it came out more like a cough. "No. It hasn't gotten that bad yet."

"Well, don't let it. You have friends. You can talk to us."

He nodded and downed some more of the coffee.

I sucked my breath in quickly as I realized something. "That's why you volunteered to work the holidays." The words tumbled out of me before I could realize I shouldn't say them, which I did, about half a second after they came out. I clapped my hand over my mouth. "Sorry, that was rude," I said through my fingers.

He shrugged it off. "It was better than spending them alone. Or with Sandra's family, trying to act like everything was okay."

"I'm so sorry," I said again. And then, before I could stop myself, "Do you think there's any chance you'll get back together?" I cringed as soon as I said it. With the way my mouth was running so much faster than my brain, I really needed to reconsider how much espresso I was drinking.

"I hope so," he said. "I'm going to try anyway."

"Just don't send her new boyfriend a million text messages hoping to scare him off." My eyes got big as I realized what I was saying before I even finished saying it. "Sorry, sorry, I was thinking about Sammy and trying to make a joke. Sorry."

"Do I need to ask you if you've been drinking?"

"I'm not. It's just too much stress and caffeine making me make bad decisions."

He nodded. "Well, you better get those under

control if you're going to help Sammy." The emotional part of our conversation was clearly over. I wasn't sure if he was glad to be moving on, but I sure was. I was a lot less likely to stick my foot in my mouth talking about Sammy's case than Mike's personal life.

"So, since the Chief of Police called in the State Police," I said, choosing my words carefully—it was a lot easier when I wasn't talking about marriages breaking up, apparently—"Does that mean you won't be able to help me figure out who really killed Cheryl?"

He eyed me, back in full professional mode. "I was never helping you, Fran. You were interfering in my investigation, remember?"

I put on a dramatic thinking face and tapped a finger against my chin. "No, that doesn't sound familiar."

He rolled his eyes and took another slug of his coffee. "Somehow, I'm not surprised."

I grinned and then remembered whose case we were talking about. "But seriously, Mike, between friends. I can't leave this alone. You know that."

His head moved slightly in what I thought and chose to believe was a nod.

"I'm going to do whatever I can to prove she's innocent."

His head twitched again.

"You know she's innocent, too."

Twitch.

"Will you help me?"

This time, he closed his eyes and took a long, deep breath. "It's not my case anymore, Fran."

"But it should be."

This time, an eyebrow twitched.

"Mike, help me figure out who really killed Cheryl. Prove to the Chief that you're a better detective than this MSP guy."

"He's one of their top detectives."

"I'm trying to help you here, Mike."

The corner of his mouth twitched.

"Will you help me?"

"I gotta tell you, Fran, Dick's not going to like you getting involved in his case, and he's sure not going to like me interfering."

"Dick? Who's Dick?"

"The MSP detective. Dick Philips."

"His name's Dick? Not Richard? Or Rich? Or Rick?" I ran out of other, better names he could have used before I ran out of incredulity that he chose to go by Dick.

"I guess he thinks it sounds like a good detective name. Dick Tracy and all."

"Yeah, but still." I shook my head. "Anyway, I don't care if he doesn't like me getting involved. He doesn't know Sammy and he doesn't know Cape Bay. This is my friend and my town, and I'm going to investigate it. Will you help me?"

He looked at me for a few seconds, then drained

his coffee cup. Seriously, how did he drink that much coffee that fast? "You know I can't do that."

"I'll take that as a maybe."

He definitely almost smiled. "I gotta warn you, Fran. You need to be careful. Dick's tough. He's a take-no-prisoners kind of guy."

"But isn't that the whole point of being a detective? To take prisoners?"

Mike outright laughed. "Yeah, Fran, I guess it is. I guess it is."

Chapter 10

SAMMY SHOWED up at the café about an hour after Mike left. "I can't just sit around the house all day. It's making me antsy. I need to keep busy. I need—" She stopped as she finally looked around the café. "There's no one here."

"Nope. Slow day," I replied.

"Hey! I'm here!" Rhonda called from a corner where she was curled up with her romance novel. She'd clocked out a while earlier, but stayed for the comfortable chair and coffee.

Sammy called hello to her, then turned back to me. "Has it been like this all day?"

"Pretty much. Mike came in a while ago, but otherwise, it's just been me and Rhonda. I've been getting a lot of cleaning done."

"I bet. Is there anything left for me to do?"

I looked around. "You could update the menu

boards, I guess." The chalkboard menus above the counter were still adorned with Christmas trees and Santa Claus. Updating them hadn't really been high on my to-do list but since everything was pretty clean and we had no customers, there wasn't much else for her to do. At the same time, mentioning Mike's visit had reminded me of what he'd said. I wondered if she knew yet what they had found.

My thoughts must have shown on my face.

"What? What is it?" Sammy asked.

I shifted uncomfortably.

"Fran?" Fear showed on her face.

"Has Ryan told you…" I trailed off, not really wanting to be the bearer of bad news. I hoped with my prompt she'd volunteer that Ryan had already told her about the DNA. He had to know, didn't he? Or would they have kept it from him?

"Told me what?"

I glanced over at Rhonda who was unconvincingly pretending not to be eavesdropping. She was probably eavesdropping when I was talking to Mike too. Maybe she would volunteer to tell Sammy? She wasn't moving, so I finally tilted my head towards the back room. "Let's go back there."

Sammy's face got a little paler.

"Rhonda, could you keep an eye on things out here?"

"Sure!" She jumped up so fast that any thought I

had that maybe she really was reading promptly disappeared.

Rhonda came to take my place behind the counter and I led Sammy into the back room. She stood in the middle of the room anxiously, clasping and squeezing her hands. "Sit down," I said.

That seemed to scare her even more, but she sat. Fortunately, there was a chair right behind her and she didn't have to go far for it. She looked so shaky I wasn't sure she would have made it.

I grabbed another chair and pulled it over close enough that our knees were almost touching when I sat down. And then I leaned towards her with my elbows on my knees. "Sammy—" I took a deep breath. I had to tell her. "They found DNA on Cheryl's body. *Your* DNA."

She stared at me for a long time, to the point that I wondered if maybe she somehow hadn't heard me. When she did respond, her voice came out as a breath. "What?" Then she repeated it louder. "What? But I never—I never touched her. I never even saw her after that day you kicked her out! She couldn't—I didn't—Fran, it's not possible!" She was frantic. She was up out of her chair, looking around with an expression that I could only describe as terror. "What am I going to do? I didn't kill her! I didn't touch her! Why do they think—how can they think—?"

I stood up and took her by the shoulders. "Take a breath."

She did, but didn't seem any calmer.

"Deep breath," I said slowly. "Deep breath."

She listened and calmed down a little, at least enough that I felt like she would hear me if I talked to her.

"First of all, I believe you. We all believe you."

"But then why—"

I shook my head. "Nobody who knows you thinks you could have done it. They just... have to look at the evidence."

"But why is my—"

"That's what we're going to figure out. You and me. Okay? You and me, we're going to figure out why your DNA was on Cheryl's body."

Sammy nodded and I took that as a good sign.

"Now, can you think of any way it could have happened? Did you touch her coat or anything when she was in here?" Mike hadn't mentioned where on Cheryl's body they'd found the DNA, but her coat seemed like as good a place as any.

Sammy shook her head. "No. No, I don't think so."

"Okay, where else? Where else could your DNA have been? How else could she have gotten it on her?"

"I don't know," Sammy said, looking frantic again.

"Sammy, take a deep breath and—" It came to us both at the same time.

"My apartment!"

"Have you been back there since New Year's?"

She shook her head furiously. "I didn't want to be alone. I was too creeped out, especially after that text she sent."

"If she was actually in your apartment, there are probably all kinds of ways she could have gotten your DNA on her."

"That's—that's—I don't even want to think about that. Her pawing around in my things, touching them, rubbing them on her?" She shuddered.

I didn't blame her. The idea of someone invading my personal space like that gave me the willies. But if we could provide an alternate explanation for why Cheryl had Sammy's DNA on her, that would go a long way towards getting Sammy off the hook. "We need to go to your apartment. We need to look around and see if we can tell that she was there."

Sammy looked skeptical. "Really, Fran? I mean—"

I cut her off. "You can't stay at Ryan's forever. Well, you can, but you'll want your stuff. You have to go back sooner or later, and it may as well be sooner." I grabbed my coat off the hook before she could say anything else and walked back out into the café. "Rhonda, can you keep an eye on things here? Sammy and I are going out for a little bit."

"Sure thing!" She waved in my general direction without looking up from her book.

Sammy followed me reluctantly. I almost felt bad making her come with me, but I needed her. I'd never been to her apartment before and wouldn't have a clue if something was out of place. She had to come.

It was a short walk over to her place. She lived in an apartment over one of the shops on Main Street, just a couple of blocks from Antonia's. The stairs were in the back, so we circled around the building. I glanced around while Sammy unlocked the door, and I felt a little shiver go down my spine, and not just because of the icy breeze that managed to find its way under my coat. It was the middle of the day and we were the only two people in sight. The shop under Sammy's apartment—a beachwear shop—was closed for the season. No wonder Sammy hadn't wanted to come back here.

She swung the door open but stood back from it.

"Want me to go first?"

She nodded.

I stepped past her and headed up the stairs. At the top was another locked door. Sammy handed me the keys and I opened it up. "How could she have gotten through two locked doors?" I muttered.

"I forget to lock them sometimes. It's Cape Bay. I don't worry about it too much."

I shook my head. I never locked a door in my life until I moved to New York City and found out that most places weren't like Cape Bay. Most places, people lock their doors. Once I got used to it, it made so much sense that I kept it up when I moved back home and didn't understand why everyone didn't do it.

"Well, I guess you remembered the other night," I said, opening the door. "Maybe she wasn't here after all." On the one hand, I was sure Sammy would be reassured to know that Cheryl hadn't been in her apartment after all. On the other hand, Cheryl being there was the key to Sammy's DNA being on her body.

"Yeah, I guess," Sammy replied. She didn't exactly sound confident.

"You guess?"

"Well…"

I waited, my hand still resting on the doorknob.

"When Ryan picked me up that night, I forgot my phone and had to go back inside for it. I don't remember taking my keys with me."

"Maybe you locked it by hand?"

"They're deadbolts, Fran. You need the key."

I looked at the door and realized she was right. There was no way to lock it from the outside without the key. "So either you're remembering wrong or—"

"How would she have gotten a key?"

"I don't know. I don't want to think about it. I'm so creeped out right now, Fran. I don't—can we just go back to the café?"

For a moment, I wanted to agree. But, more than that, I knew we had to find out if Cheryl had been in Sammy's apartment. If we could find proof that

Cheryl could have gotten Sammy's DNA on her somehow other than Sammy killing her, we had to do it. All we had to do was find it and Sammy would be off the hook. "No. We have to do this." I stepped into the apartment. The lights were off and the curtains were closed, so I could barely see.

Sammy flipped the light on. "Everything looks—" She stopped mid-sentence.

"Everything looks what?"

"My scarf is gone."

"Sammy, it's on your neck."

"Not that one. This one! The one that goes with this coat." She touched the collar of a coat hanging from a hook on the wall. She squeezed the coat's pocket. "My gloves are gone, too."

"You couldn't have lost them somewhere?"

"No, I know it was here before I left because I thought about wearing that coat instead."

I nodded, making a mental note of the missing items. Sammy would have worn both of them against her skin, transferring some of her DNA to them, and potentially to Cheryl's body. "What else? Is anything else missing or out of place?"

Sammy looked around, then wandered around the living room and kitchen. "No, I think everything else is normal."

"Okay, let's check the bedroom."

She halted in her tracks. "But if nothing else is wrong out here—"

"Do you really think she would have come in, taken your scarf and gloves, and walked right out?"

"I guess not." Her voice came out in a strained whisper.

I really did feel bad for her having to face up to the possibility of a crazy woman having gone through her apartment on top of being accused of murdering that same crazy woman, but we had to keep going. I led the way to the bedroom.

Inside, Sammy's bed was unmade and the sheets were rumpled. There was a pile of clothes on the floor. I tried to avert my eyes and not look at the mess. Even though I was there to help her, I felt weird being in the room when she clearly hadn't planned on me being there. It felt like an invasion of privacy.

"This is *not* how I left it," Sammy said emphatically. "Look at this! My bed's a mess! And my clothes!" She grabbed a handful of clothing from the floor before I slapped her hand back down.

"Don't touch anything!"

Startled, she dropped everything and looked at me like I'd slapped her across the face instead of just swatting her hand.

"We need to be able to tell the police we didn't touch anything. We need to leave everything exactly the way it is."

She looked at me uneasily, and I could tell that she was fighting her instinct to clean up.

"Other than the bed and the clothes, is anything else different than how you left it?"

She looked around without moving since any path she had was strewn with clothing. "No, I don't think so."

"What about the bathroom?"

She picked her way across the floor to the bathroom and let out a little scream.

"What? What is it?" I jumped across the pile of clothes and crashed into Sammy's back.

One hand clapped over her mouth, she pointed with the other.

Scrawled across the mirror in giant, lipstick-red letters were the words "Hi Sammy!" surrounded by lip prints.

"I take it that wasn't here before?"

"No!"

I stepped cautiously past her, careful not to touch anything. There was makeup strewn all across the counter, along with a couple of brushes, a comb, and some hair spray. If I was honest, it didn't look too different from how my bathroom looked when I was late getting ready to leave before a night out. Except for the lipstick message across the mirror, of course. "Was all this out when you left?"

She shook her head in the mirror.

"But it's all yours?"

She nodded.

"Even the lipstick?" I'd spotted a tube in the sink,

all the way open and blunted on the end from writing on the mirror. By the smears of bright red in the sink, it looked like Cheryl had just dropped it when she finished.

She leaned over to look, then nodded. "But it doesn't look good on me. I never wear it."

Even if it had looked good on her, I didn't think she'd be wearing it anymore since it was more of a stub now than an actual lipstick. I stood back and looked around from the bathroom to the bedroom. "Well, I guess it's safe to say that we found a few ways Cheryl could have gotten your DNA on her."

Sammy looked at me curiously.

"Your scarf, your gloves, your clothes, your lipstick."

Sammy shivered. Her apartment was a little cold, but I didn't think that was why.

"Come on," I said. "Let's get out of here."

She nodded. "I guess we need to call Mike and let him know, huh?"

"Mike's not on the case anymore," I said absently as I closed the door behind us, locking it firmly. It still bothered me that Sammy said she hadn't locked her doors, but they'd been locked when we arrived. How was that possible? Maybe Sammy had remembered wrong? Or maybe they'd been unlocked when we arrived and we just hadn't noticed?

"What?" Sammy sounded shocked, but I didn't know why.

"What what?" I asked, turning around and looking back at her. She'd stopped dead in the middle of the street, but I'd kept walking.

"Mike's not on the case anymore?"

"Did I say that out loud?"

"Yes!"

Darn it. I'd meant to break it to her gently. I knew she—all of us—felt like with Mike on the case, Sammy was safe. He knew she wasn't capable of murdering anyone. I sighed. Now that I'd accidentally spilled the beans, I may as well fill her in. "The Chief of police called in the State Police to investigate. Some guy named Dick Phillips is in charge of the case now."

"Are you serious? Fran, if you're joking around, you need to tell me right now!" Her voice shook even though she was obviously trying to keep it together. I walked back towards her.

"I wouldn't joke about that. I'm sorry."

Sammy covered her face with her hands as she fought back tears. "What am I going to do, Fran? What am I going to do? I can't—I can't go to jail!"

I put my hands on her shoulders. "You're not going to jail, okay? Mike said this new guy is one of the State Police's top detectives. I'm sure he'll find a new suspect in no time flat and you'll be off the hook."

"You think so?" she asked, sniffling.

"I know so," I said, more confidently than maybe

I felt. I needed to keep it up for Sammy's sake though. So I doubled down. "In fact, I bet he'll already be interrogating a suspect down at the police station tomorrow. You have nothing to worry about."

I was at least partially right. Dick Phillips did have a suspect at the police station for an interrogation the next day. The only problem was it was Sammy.

Chapter 11

IT SOUNDED innocent enough at first—Detective Phillips called Sammy up and asked her to go down to the station to go over a few things with him. She said that the way he said it made it sound almost like he just wanted to have a little chat. When she called me to ask if I could cover her at the café, she said he told her he wanted to hear her side of the story, so he could understand the case better.

"Are you taking Giorgio DiGiorgio?" I asked.

"The lawyer? No, I wasn't planning on it. Detective Phillips said he just had a couple of quick questions for me. I wouldn't want to bother Giorgio with that."

"Are you sure? Didn't he say you weren't supposed to talk to Mike at all unless he was there?"

"I didn't really think he meant I shouldn't *ever* talk to him. He just wanted to be there if I was officially being questioned. And I'm not. Detective Phillips just wants to go over a couple of things."

I wasn't so sure about that. "Have you told Ryan about this?" He was a cop. He would know if Phillips was just looking to have a friendly chat.

"I called him, but he didn't answer, so I just left him a voicemail to let him know I'd be down there if he wanted to get lunch or something after."

I wondered if I should call Mike to ask his opinion."

"Hang on a second. Oh, that's Ryan calling on the other line. Let me call you right back, Fran."

Sammy hung up, and I waited by the phone for a few seconds, wondering what I should do. I had just decided that I may as well get dressed for work since I had to go into the café soon either way when the phone rang. It was Sammy again. This time, she sounded a little less confident than before.

"Ryan said that under absolutely no circumstances should I talk to Detective Phillips without Giorgio DiGiorgio there, so I called him and he's going to meet me at the station in half an hour."

I breathed a sigh of relief. Even if Giorgio DiGiorgio didn't actually *need* to be there, I felt better knowing that he would be. Sammy could be so innocent and trusting that I wasn't actually sure that she'd know if a detective was trying to trick her into saying something she shouldn't.

"Can you be here to cover the café for me by then?"

"Of course," I said, getting up from my kitchen table where I'd been lingering over another eggnog latte when she called. "I'll be there in twenty minutes."

One of the great things about living in a very small town was that I could get dressed and make it into work in twenty minutes, and the ten minutes Sammy would have left before she was due to meet Giorgio DiGiorgio would be more than she needed to get there on time.

Twenty minutes later, I was in the café and Sammy was out the door with a promise to let me know how it went. The time ticked by. First an hour, then two hours, then three. Shouldn't she have been done by now? Maybe she just forget to call. Should I just call her? What if she was still talking to Detective Phillips? She'd probably have her phone on silent, but what if she didn't? I didn't want to interrupt. Finally, I decided to text her: "How's the meeting with Phillips going?"

Another hour went by. I wondered if I should call Mike to see if he knew anything. I decided to wait.

After another hour, I couldn't take it anymore. I picked up the phone. Before I could dial, I heard the café's back door open. "Sammy?" I hurried into the back room. "Sammy?"

She was sitting in a chair at the little table, her head in her hands.

"Sammy, what's wrong?"

"I'm going to jail," she said quietly.

"What? No you're not. I told you, Detective Phillips—"

She looked up at me, her blue eyes rimmed with red. "Detective Phillips thinks I killed Cheryl."

"I'm sure he—"

"Trust me, Fran. He told me. He spent two hours telling me how he thinks I killed her and all the evidence he has that will prove it."

"Two hours? But you were gone—"

"Giorgio and I went back to his office and went over it all again. And again. He had me tell him what happened three times. He asked me so many questions I started to wonder if I was remembering things wrong. Not the big stuff, like whether I killed her, but whether I saw her again after the day you kicked her out. Or if maybe I left my gloves and scarf somewhere by accident. But I didn't. I know I didn't." Tears started to fill her eyes. "Giorgio said they probably have enough for an arrest warrant, or close to it. I'm scared, Fran. I'm really scared."

I sat down next to her and took her hand, not knowing what else to do. "We'll get through this. I promise you. We'll get through this."

She inhaled a very shaky breath. "How do you know?"

"I don't know. I just do." And I did. Sammy going to jail was an impossibility. It wouldn't happen—*couldn't* happen. And if this new detective was set on proving Sammy was the murderer, I was just going to have to prove that she wasn't. And, to do that, I had to know more about Cheryl. "Cheryl was from up in Plymouth, right?"

Sammy nodded. "She and Ryan grew up there."

"So if she lived up there, how did she get down here?"

Sammy looked at me like I was crazy. It wasn't like it was hard to travel from one town to another.

"I mean, did she drive, take the bus, what? If she drove, where's her car? If she took the bus, the bus doesn't run at night, especially not on New Year's. Did she have a place to stay for the night or was she planning to lurk around outside all night?" I tried not to think about the possibility that she had planned to stay in Sammy's apartment.

"Ryan said she didn't have a license. It got suspended too many times, and she eventually just gave up."

That doesn't mean she's not still driving, I thought. I didn't think I should say it out loud though. "So the bus," I did say. "Other than Ryan, did she know anyone in town?" Before I could say anything else, the bell over the front door jingled. "Hold that thought." I started towards the door out to the café, then turned around. "We should check with Ed Martin over at the

Surfside Inn. Cheryl could have been staying there." I walked out into the café and found Mike and Ryan standing at the counter.

"Sammy back there?" Ryan asked before I could even say hello.

I nodded. "Have you talked to her?"

"Just texted. I heard it was pretty rough though."

"Go on back. What do you want to drink?"

"One of those eggnog lattes. Extra espresso, please. I haven't been sleeping much."

"Coming up." I glanced over my shoulder at Mike. I didn't have to ask him anything. "I'll start a fresh pot for you," I said, dumping out the pot of plain drip coffee that had been sitting on the warmer since before I came in.

Mike made a noise that I interpreted as a "thank you" as I started the fresh pot. "How's she doing?" he asked when I turned around to make Ryan's latte.

"Not great." I answered quietly even though Ryan had closed the door behind him. "Is it as bad as she says?"

"It's not good. As far as I can tell, he's not even looking for other suspects."

I grimaced as I steamed the eggnog for Ryan's latte. "What do we need to do?"

Mike raised an eyebrow. "We?"

"Oh, stop it, Mike. I know I'm a civilian, and I'm supposed to stay out of it, but I can't just let my friend go to jail because some state cop is too lazy to look for another suspect."

Mike raised his eyebrow and glanced towards the door. A man I didn't recognize, dressed in a suit, with a close-cropped haircut and mustache was standing just outside. With a look like that, I didn't have to be told that he was a cop. And since I knew all the officers in the Cape Bay police department, I could guess who he was.

"Phillips?" I whispered to Mike as the man opened the door.

Mike grunted. I took it as a yes.

"Hello! Welcome to Antonia's!" I said as cheerfully as I could.

Phillips looked at Mike. "Stanton," he said.

"Phillips," Mike said back.

"What can I get you?" I asked. "Our menu board's right up there, but if there's something you'd like that you don't see, I'd be happy—"

"Don't you have normal coffee?" he interrupted. "I don't know why places don't just have normal coffee anymore. All these frou-frou drinks. No wonder this country's getting soft! Everybody dumping sugar in everything! Can't just drink normal coffee like a real man."

I bit my tongue to keep from saying anything catty about his "real man" comment. Instead, I forced myself to be as gracious as my grandparents would have wanted me to be.

"We have regular drip coffee, too. Actually, that's what Mike gets—plain black coffee. I just started a fresh pot." I wished now that I hadn't been so quick to dump the old pot down the sink, but serving that to him wouldn't have been grandparent-approved customer service either.

"A coffee then. Room for cream and sugar."

I wanted to remind him about sugar making the country soft, but I didn't. Aside from what my grandparents would have wanted, it probably wasn't a good idea to antagonize the man responsible for investigating Sammy.

I grabbed cups for him and Mike. As I turned around, the door to the back room opened. I shot a look in that direction, hoping to get Sammy and Ryan's attention before they came out, but it was too late.

"I should have known this is where you worked," Phillips said. "And of course Leary is holed up in the back with the suspect."

"She's my girlfriend," Ryan said coolly. Any other time, I would have been thrilled to hear him say it out loud, but I was a little distracted at the moment.

Phillips scoffed and looked dead at Mike. "This is why your Chief brought me in, you know. It's a wonder you people get any cases solved around here."

Mike's jaw clenched, but, to his credit, he didn't explode at Phillips.

I handed Phillips his coffee. "Is there anything else

I can get for you?" I asked politely.

"I don't think so," he scoffed, and reached into his jacket pocket for his wallet.

"Oh, no, sir. Police don't have to pay." I didn't want to say it, but my grandfather would have rolled over in his grave if I didn't. Besides, my grandmother had sworn by "kill them with kindness."

"A bribe? I don't think so," he snorted. He pulled out two dollars and tossed them on the counter.

"It's only one," I said, handing one back. I pointed up at where the price for plain coffee was written on the menu for good measure.

He snatched the dollar away from me and stuffed it back in his pocket, then turned on his heel and walked out without a word.

"Wow," I muttered under my breath. I filled up Mike's cup and passed it to him. "Not a bribe, I promise."

He made a noise that sounded vaguely like laughter.

"Is he always like that?" I asked.

"Friendly and sociable?" Mike replied. "Yup, sure is."

Ryan nodded. Sammy, sticking close to him, looked uncomfortable.

"And he's one of their best," I said. It came out sounding more like a statement than a question.

"A winning personality isn't one of the job requirements," Mike replied.

"If it was, ol' Stanton here would be out of a job," Ryan cracked.

Mike shot a glare Ryan's way. "Watch it, Leary. I may not be on this case, but I'm still your commanding officer."

"Yes sir!" he replied, without quite the level of seriousness Mike expected. Mike let it go though. He took a long swig from his coffee cup. Coffee cured all Mike's ills. Well, not quite *all* of them. But almost all.

I handed Ryan his latte and topped off Mike's coffee. "Can I get you guys anything else?" They both declined.

Mike headed for the door, but Ryan stopped to give Sammy a hug. When he came towards me, at first I thought he was going to hug me, too, but then he put his hand out. Strange, but less strange than him hugging me. I put my hand out too and he slapped it with his own, leaving something in my palm. I looked down. It was a half-crumbled napkin. "Uh, thanks Ryan."

"You're welcome," he replied, but something in his voice made me clutch the napkin instead of immediately dropping it in the trash. As soon as they were out the door, I looked at it. Nothing on the first side. I flipped it over. A name: Bonnie Harmon. And an address, just a couple of blocks away.

"What is it?" Sammy asked, coming over to look at it. "Who's Bonnie Harmon?"

"I don't know. But I think we need to find out."

Chapter 12

A FEW HOURS LATER, after we closed the café, Sammy and I were standing on the street, looking at the little white house with cobalt blue shutters. They were either recently painted or whoever lived here was devoted to home maintenance because a color like that didn't last long here between our salty sea air and harsh winters. I pulled my coat tighter around me as I remembered that my own house needed repainting. At least that could wait until spring. Or summer. Or maybe next fall.

"What do we do now?" Sammy asked.

"We knock on the door," I said and started up the front walk.

I'd told Sammy she didn't have to come, but she insisted. She wanted to know who Bonnie Harmon was and why Ryan gave me her address as much as I did. Maybe more since we both thought it had something to do with Cheryl's murder. She'd texted Ryan to ask about it, but his response had been a non-answer: *There was something written on the napkin?* So I texted him: *Why did you give me that napkin?* His response to me was only slightly more helpful: *So you could take care of it*

None of his answers actually admitted giving me anything other than a piece of trash, but they didn't deny it either.

So now Sammy and I were standing in front of Bonnie Harmon's cute little house, trying to work up the courage to knock on the door. What if we were completely wrong? What if Ryan really had been handing it to me to throw out? I wished I'd taken five minutes to look the name and address up online. 123 First Street wasn't exactly an unusual address. In fact, it sounded almost made up. I thought about turning around, but looked at Sammy and remembered that she was being investigated for murder.

I marched up the front walk and knocked on the door. Sammy lingered behind me.

I could hear movement inside, but it took a minute for anyone to answer. I was just about to knock again when the door swung open. I stood there for a second, staring at the woman who stood there. She was fairly average looking, but pretty, with dark hair, parted in the middle, and pulled back on the sides, wearing a blue sweater and jeans. But it was her eyes that had me transfixed. They were the brightest shade of blue I'd ever seen.

"Can I help you?" she asked in a soft southern accent.

"Um, yes," I said, struggling to collect myself as she looked at me with those exceptionally blue eyes. "Are you Bonnie Harmon?"

"I am."

"My name's Francesca Amaro—Fran. This may be a long shot, but—" I paused and took a breath. "Do you happen to know a woman named Cheryl?"

She instantly tensed up. "I'm sure I know a Cheryl or two. Is there a certain one you're looking for?"

I didn't believe for a second that she needed to ask if we were looking for a certain Cheryl. But I was going to have to play along if I was going to get her to help us. "Cheryl, uh—" I tried to remember if I'd ever heard Cheryl's last name.

"Darling," Sammy whispered from behind me. "Cheryl Darling."

"Cheryl Darling," I repeated, glad Sammy'd said Cheryl's full name. Before she did, I briefly thought she was calling *me* darling. "About my height, blonde hair, brown eyes, thin."

Bonnie jutted her chin out. "I've already talked to the police. If Detective Phillips has any more questions, he can ask me himself. I'm not going to tell you anything different just because you're a woman and he's a man." She made a move like she was going to close the door, and I flung my hand out to grab the door jamb in an attempt to stop her. I realized almost immediately that my hand wouldn't do much to stop her. If anything, she'd just slam it on my fingers and then I'd let go. Valuing the use of my fingers, I dropped my hand.

"We're not the police," I said quickly.

She didn't slam the door in my face, but she didn't invite us in either.

"I'm just asking some questions—"

"I'm not talking to reporters either."

I sighed. "I'm not a reporter. I'm just—my friend —" I reached behind me and flailed around for Sammy's arm. I got it and pulled her up next to me. "This is Sammy." A look flitted across Bonnie's face, but I wasn't sure if it meant that she hadn't known Sammy was with me or something else. "Sammy—the police think Sammy killed Cheryl. She didn't!" I rushed to say that to make sure Bonnie didn't think I was asking her to invite a murderer into her home. "Sammy wouldn't hurt a fly. But that Detective Phillips you mentioned, they brought him in from the Massachusetts State Police, and he doesn't know Sammy like the rest of us do. He doesn't know she couldn't possibly have killed anyone. We're trying to learn as much as we can about Cheryl so that we can figure out who the real murderer is."

Bonnie looked at us cautiously for a few seconds. "So you want to see Cheryl's stuff?"

I hesitated for a second, then realized why Ryan had given me this address. It was where Cheryl had been staying while she was in town. "Yes, if we can."

Bonnie nodded slowly, then pushed the door open. "Come on in. The police have already been through it all, so I don't see what's the harm." She led us inside and down a short hallway. "This is the room Cheryl was staying in."

I glanced around as Sammy and I stepped inside. "Wow! You really like *Gone with the Wind*, huh? Or is all this Cheryl's?" The room was decorated with at least ten *Gone with the Wind* posters, along with several signed pictures of the stars and, if I wasn't mistaken, an exact replica of the green velvet curtains Scarlett used to make her dress in the movie.

Bonnie laughed quietly and smiled. "No, it's mine. Well, my mom's, originally. She was the real fan. I just inherited all this. I couldn't stand to put it away somewhere though, so now I live in a little shrine to *Gone with the Wind*. I sort of *am* a shrine to it, too, so I guess it's okay."

I looked at her curiously, almost afraid to know how she herself was a shrine to the movie.

"When my mom found out she was having a girl, she desperately wanted to name me after Scarlett's daughter in the movie—Bonnie Blue Butler—so she prayed day and night that I'd have blue eyes so she could name me after her."

"Don't all babies have blue eyes though?" I asked slowly.

"Sure do. Mom just lucked out that mine stuck, I guess." She laughed. "Cheryl's stuff is right over there. You're lucky you came today. I was going to take it all to the post office to ship up to her mother in Boston tomorrow morning."

She let us know she'd be in the living room and left us to it.

"What are we looking for?" Sammy asked when we were alone.

"I'm not really sure." I knelt down to unzip the faded duffel bag on the floor. "A list of her enemies, maybe? A signed confession from the killer?"

Sammy looked at me like she didn't think my jokes were funny.

"I don't know. Anything that could tell us anything about her or her life or why she was so fixated on you."

"Because I'm dating Ryan."

"About that," I said, sitting back on my heels. "When were you going to tell me that you guys were officially together?"

Sammy was suddenly very focused on the duffle bag, but I saw the flush creeping up her neck. "We wanted to take things slow. And then Christmas came, and there was the whole thing with Cheryl." She shrugged. "Everybody knew anyway. You guys have been teasing us about it for months."

"True." We finished looking through the duffle bag, then I poked around the room, looking to see if Bonnie had missed anything of Cheryl's, or if maybe Cheryl had deliberately hidden something. Nothing.

"So now what?" Sammy asked.

"Now we talk to Bonnie. Cheryl ended up staying here somehow. Let's find out how."

We found our way to the living room where Bonnie was sitting at a computer with an impressive three monitors.

"Y'all find anything?" she asked, looking up from whatever she was doing.

"Unfortunately, no," I said. "But we were hoping we could talk to you for a few minutes?"

"Sure! Let me just close out of this here." She made a few mouse clicks and minimized some windows, then turned around to us. "Sorry, I'm a free-lance graphic designer and I'm a little behind on this project. Haven't had much time to work on it with the holidays and all, so I try to get a few minutes of work in here and there wherever I can. But please, sit down. Can I get y'all anything? I still have some leftover eggnog if you want some or I can make some coffee right quick."

As much as I would have enjoyed a warm cup of coffee on such a cold night, I was always suspicious of other people's brews. Too many years making and drinking excellent coffee had made me a snob. "Some eggnog would be nice."

Sammy agreed, and Bonnie went to the kitchen to get it, coming back out a few moments later with a pitcher and three glasses arranged neatly on a tray. She even had a little shaker of nutmeg beside it. She poured our glasses, adding just a touch of nutmeg on the top of each, and handed them to us. "So what do ya'll want to know?"

I took a sip of the eggnog as I tried to think of where to start. Then I took another sip. "This is really good!"

Bonnie beamed. "Thank you!"

One more sip and I felt like my thoughts were together. "How did you know Cheryl?"

Bonnie sipped her eggnog thoughtfully. "I didn't really. I know that sounds strange with her staying in my house and all, but I actually just ran into her when I was getting lunch one day and we got to talking. She said she'd be in town for a few days and needed a place to stay, so I offered, and that's how she ended up staying in my guest room."

"That's very generous of you." Personally, I couldn't imagine inviting a total stranger to stay in my home, but apparently Bonnie was more trusting than me.

"I try to be hospitable."

I couldn't disagree, and not just because she'd let Cheryl stay with her. She'd also let me and Sammy in right after I told her that the police thought Sammy was a murderer. She either had hospitality in her blood or incredibly bad judgement. "Did you notice anything unusual about Cheryl while she was staying here?"

Bonnie sipped her eggnog. "No, not that I can think of. She kept mostly to herself. She was on her phone a lot. And she wasn't even here most of the time. She came in a couple of days before New Year's, but was really only just here to sleep. She'd go out in the morning and come back sort of later in the evening. I didn't even see much of her."

"Did she tell you why she was here?"

"No, we didn't talk about it. I got the impression she was here to see someone though. I didn't ask who it was. She didn't much seem to want to talk about it. I did think it was strange that she wasn't staying with them, but, well, I got the impression it might have been a gentleman friend that she maybe wasn't ready to spend the night with, bless her heart."

Either that or it was a gentleman who wouldn't let her into his house over his dead body, but I wasn't going to say that. Instead, I smiled. "What about you? You don't sound like you're from here."

Bonnie laughed. "No, I don't guess I do! I'm from Georgia. Atlanta, of course, if the whole *Gone with the Wind* thing didn't tip you off. My mom was actually from up this way, but she moved down to Atlanta because of how much she loved that movie."

"Wow, that's devotion!"

"Well, that's a nicer word than obsession, so, yes."

"So did you move up here to be closer to her side of the family?" I sipped some more of that tasty eggnog. It really was very good. I wondered what her secret was.

"No, they're all gone now. But I got to know the Rhode Island School of Design when we used to come up here to visit when I was a kid and always wanted to go there. After college, I got a job and just stayed."

"Have you been in Cape Bay long?"

"No, I haven't. Would y'all like any more eggnog?" She picked up the pitcher and looked at us expectantly.

"I'll have some," I said, wondering whether she was changing the subject or just trying to be polite.

She refilled my cup and her own. Sammy had barely touched hers and didn't need any more. Bonnie set the pitcher down but didn't offer any more information about how she came to be in Cape Bay. Still, I hadn't asked, so maybe it wasn't a total evasion on her part. I did feel like she was keeping something from me though. Maybe if I offered her a little information about me, she'd open up some.

"I just moved here, too," I said. "Over the summer. I'd just been through a messy breakup and then my mom died, so I came back here to nurse my wounds by the ocean and run the family café—Antonia's, down on Main Street. Have you been there?"

"I've walked by, but I haven't stopped in. I guess

I'll have to, now that I know you." She smiled warmly, and I had a feeling that no matter how this conversation turned out, I'd be seeing her again soon.

"You should come by! Sammy works for me there, too. One or the other of us is pretty much always there."

"Oh, I'll definitely have to come in then! There are so many cute little shops in town, I just haven't been able to make it everywhere!" She took another sip of her eggnog, looking like she had something on her mind. "You know, since you mentioned your breakup, it was actually a breakup that brought me here, too." She shifted uncomfortably in her chair. "My boyfriend—my ex-boyfriend, I mean—he was dating this girl before me and she left him for her ex. I thought my boyfriend was over her, but one day he told me he was going back to her, just like that. She'd decided she wanted him after all, and me, I just got thrown in the gutter." She stared down into her eggnog. When she looked up at me again, her eyes were shining with tears. "We were all in the same group of friends, and I just couldn't stand to see them together, so I picked myself up and moved. I do some work for a magazine that featured Cape Bay and thought it looked like the most precious little town that would be perfect for mending a broken heart."

I wanted to reach across and pat her hand, but my New England reserve kept me from it. Instead, I just smiled sympathetically. "The ocean's good for that.

The beach and the waves. They always make me feel better."

Bonnie nodded. "I've been spending a lot of time down on the beach. I know it's crazy in the wintertime, but, well, it just speaks to me."

"Doesn't sound crazy to me at all!" I laughed. "You, Sammy?"

She laughed too. "I would think it sounded crazier if you *didn't* like to go down to the beach in the winter. It's the best time. In the summer, there are so many tourists here that it's almost too crowded to go."

"Have you been here through a tourist season yet?" I asked.

Bonnie shook her head. "No, I just moved up a couple of months ago. Is it bad?"

"Not too bad. Just different."

We sat and talked for a little while longer. Once you got her talking, Bonnie was warm and friendly, and even kind of funny. I could tell that she really was the kind of person who would open up her home to someone who needed a place to stay, even if that person was a total stranger. Of course, there was no way she could have known that Cheryl was a crazy stalker who was determined to make Sammy's life miserable, so I didn't hold it against her.

We finally said our goodbyes with Sammy and me bundling ourselves up to go back out in the frigid cold. The wind had picked up, so it felt even colder than when we'd arrived. We extracted a promise from

Bonnie to come by the café, and stepped out onto Bonnie's front step. Almost as soon as the door closed, I heard a sniffle come from Sammy. At first, I thought it was just from the cold, but then there was another and another. I looked at her and saw tears spilling out of her eyes onto her cheeks.

Chapter 13

"SAMMY, WHAT'S WRONG?" I was surprised to see Sammy crying and, on top of that, afraid that her tears would freeze to her cheeks if she didn't stop. She just stood there, sniffling, so I quickly wiped her cheeks with gloved hand, then took her arm and led her down Bonnie's front walk so we weren't just lingering on her front steps. "Sammy, tell me what's wrong," I repeated.

"I'm just so scared, Fran." She sniffed and wiped at her nose with her glove. "We're nowhere! Nowhere! When Ryan gave you Bonnie's address, I thought it had to be something important, that Bonnie would know something or be the murderer or something, but she doesn't and she's not! And she's so nice on top of it that I feel guilty for thinking she might be!"

I guided her down the street a few steps. "It's okay, Sammy. Look, we found out where Cheryl was staying, didn't we? And we got to ask Bonnie a few questions about her. I know it doesn't feel like much progress, but it is. We're further than we were an hour ago. If it was as easy as talking to one person, the police would have the case solved by now. We have to keep going."

Sammy sniffled again and wiped her face. Her breathing was still ragged, but I could tell she was at least trying to calm down.

"Come on." I took her arm and led her down the sidewalk. "Are you going back to Ryan's tonight?"

She nodded.

"Do you need to go by your place to get anything?"

She shook her head. "Ryan told me not to until they come search it."

"Are they going to?"

"After I told him what we found, he said he was going to try to get them to."

Try didn't sound as certain as I wanted it to. It was like Phillips didn't believe that Cheryl had been harassing Sammy, like he thought Sammy was making the whole thing up. I gritted my teeth together. I had to figure out some way to kick this investigation into gear. I needed to know more about Cheryl. And with Bonnie being more or less a dead end, I had to find someone else who would know about Cheryl. One person came immediately to mind. "Will Ryan be home when you get there?"

Sammy pulled out her phone and looked at the time. "He should be."

"Think he'd mind talking to me for a little while?"

"I'm sure he'd be happy to."

We walked to Ryan's house in relative silence. We both had a lot on our minds, probably Sammy even more than me. Her case weighed on me though. I spent the whole walk thinking about what I could do to help her.

Ryan's house wasn't far—it was Cape Bay, after all, but we were frozen to the bone by the time we got there.

"Coffee?" Sammy asked after calling out to let Ryan know we'd come in.

I nodded as I tried to keep my teeth from chattering. I was so cold, I probably would have willingly drunk gas station coffee if it was offered to me. Not that I expected coffee that Sammy made with Ryan's equipment to be gas station quality, just that it wouldn't have mattered. She could have served me hot water and I'd have knocked it back without a second thought.

Ryan, having apparently been home long enough to warm up since he was wearing a pair of basketball shorts and nothing else, walked out of his bedroom and into the living room where I was standing. For a few long seconds, he stared at me. Then, with the calm of a hostage negotiator, he said, "Fran. I didn't know you were here. I'll be right back." Then he turned around and walked out of the room. When he came back a minute later, he was wearing a long sleeve t-shirt and a pair of track pants, as though, having just shown me so very much skin, he now wanted to cover it all up.

"Did you get cold?" I asked wryly.

His face turned bright red. "Uh, yeah," he said and looked at the floor. He was cute. No wonder Sammy liked him.

Sammy walked back in the room holding two cups of coffee. It smelled so good my mouth started watering, and my hands almost felt warm in anticipation of holding the mug. She handed one to me and I clutched it close to my chest with both hands.

Sammy smiled at Ryan. "Oh good, you heard us come in! I yelled for you, but I wasn't sure you heard me. I was afraid you'd show up in your underwear or something if you didn't know Fran was here."

I couldn't help it. I burst out laughing.

Ryan turned even redder.

"What? What did I miss?" Sammy asked. She looked at Ryan. "You didn't walk out in your underwear, did you?"

I was laughing so hard I had to put the coffee cup down. Ryan looked like he wanted to melt into the floor.

"What? Tell me!"

"It wasn't his underwear," I managed finally. "They were real shorts."

"Really?" Sammy looked at me like she thought I was making it up.

I nodded. Ryan covered his face with his hands.

She looked at him. "You really walked out here in just a pair of basketball shorts?"

He nodded, his head still in his hands.

For a second, Sammy didn't say anything. Then she burst out laughing too. She laughed so hard she fell down on the couch. Ryan just stood there, turning six shades of red. When his shoulders started to shake, I was afraid he was starting to cry. But then I realized he was laughing too, which made me laugh harder. The three of us laughed, and laughed at each other laughing until the chill came off my bones and I realized my coffee was getting cold. I grabbed the cup and sucked it down. It was just on the right side of too cold. Not hot enough anymore that it would have warmed me up, but the laughter had taken care of that, so I didn't mind. I still wanted another, warmer, cup though.

"Sammy, is there any more coffee left?"

"Yes, would you like me to get you some?"

"No, I can get it." I went to the kitchen and poured myself a second cup. I probably wouldn't be able to sleep tonight, but, despite the laugher, Sammy's case was still at the forefront of my mind, and I didn't really think I'd be sleeping much anyway. I took a couple of sips from the cup as I waited there in the kitchen for a minute to let Ryan and Sammy have a few seconds alone. Then, walking louder than I normally would, I walked back towards the living room. I loudly bumped into a kitchen chair for good measure. "So, Ryan, do you think I could ask you a few questions about Cheryl?" I asked loudly as I walked into the room, staring at my feet as I walked.

Even after all that, the two of them were still just jumping apart when I looked up. They both blushed and I just shook my head.

"Uh, what was that you asked, Fran?" Ryan wiped his hand across his mouth like he was making sure he didn't have any trace of Sammy's lipstick on his lips. She wasn't wearing any though, so he was safe.

"I was just wondering if you could tell me a little more Cheryl. What she was like back when you knew her and all. I'm trying to get a better understanding of her so I can figure out who might have had a motive to kill her."

Ryan flicked a glance at Sammy and nodded. "Have you found any leads yet?"

I wanted to ask him if he had since he was the police detective and all, but I didn't. I knew he was being kept out of the case, or at least as out of it as he could be in a tiny police department. He was doing his best to help us by talking to me—and slipping me that note earlier.

"Well, I did come across a name and address for a woman named Bonnie Harmon—" I gave him a pointed look even though the three of us were alone in Ryan's house. "—that looked promising. It turned out to be a woman Cheryl was staying with for a few days before she died. Sammy and I talked to her for a while and she was nice, but we didn't really learn a whole lot that was useful." I met his eyes and held them for a few seconds. This was his moment to indicate to me somehow if that was all I was supposed to have gotten out of my visit to Bonnie or if there was something else.

He held my gaze, nodded slightly, then asked me what else I wanted to know.

"Who Cheryl's friends were, for starters."

Ryan nodded.

"And then who her enemies were, if you know."

"You got a while? That's not going to be a short list."

"I have as much time as it will take you to tell me," I replied, sitting down on the couch to show how ready I was to stay for as long as the conversation took. Thankfully, I'd asked Matt to take care of Latte as soon as I realized I needed to go to Bonnie's after I got done at the café. Not that I needed to ask. Matt and Latte were devoted to each other, and I'd even known Matt to go over to check on Latte if I was going to be just fifteen minutes late. At least that was the excuse he used.

"It's been a long time since I've lived in Plymouth," Ryan said, sitting down in a chair facing me. "I'm not going to know everyone she'd been hanging out with lately."

"But you'll know enough to get me started. And you still have connections up there who can help me fill in the blanks."

He nodded, then got up and disappeared down the hall. I looked at Sammy. She shrugged. A moment later, Ryan reappeared carrying a small spiral-bound notebook and pen. He handed them to me. "You'll want to take notes."

Chapter 14

I DID TAKE NOTES. A lot of notes. And I spent the next day working through them, calling people whose numbers Ryan had given me, then calling the people they mentioned. It was slow going, especially since I was doing it in between customers at the café. On top of that, it seemed like over the years, most of Ryan's friends had fallen out of touch with Cheryl, many of them on purpose.

"She stole my boyfriend."

"She started calling my girlfriend at all hours of the night."

"I couldn't go out in public with her without her making a big scene."

"She thought everyone was flirting with her and then either threw herself at them or got mad that they dared to be interested in her."

I heard what felt like a million different reasons

people had stopped being friends with her, but they all seemed to boil down to one thing: she was crazy.

A lot of the people I called talked to me, but plenty of people hung up on me too. Some because, according to them, they never wanted to hear Cheryl's name again, but some clearly did it because they were still close to her and weren't going to talk about their friend to some stranger. I put stars beside the names of those people. I needed to find a way to get them to talk to me. A couple people sounded emotional talking about her, and one girl even broke into tears. Those people I put two stars next to. I *really* wanted to talk to those people some more.

But by the end of the day, after calling more people in a few hours than I'd called in the entire month before, I didn't feel like I was much further along than I had been after talking to Ryan the night before. Sure, I knew a little more about Cheryl than I had before—she inspired very strong reactions in people, for one—but it wasn't enough that I felt like I had a clue who hated her enough to want her dead. There were people who hated her, yes, and people who didn't exactly sound sad she was dead, but I still didn't know who could have killed her.

Feeling somewhat dejected, I cleaned up the café and closed it down for the night. I was craving tacos and thought about stopping by the little Mexican restaurant down on the beach, but it was still frigid outside and I had walked to the café.

Instead I just texted Matt: *On my way. Craving tacos!!! Is that what you're making me for dinner? Lol*

I followed it with a series of smilie faces that made it clear that I was joking. He would have known anyway. Cooking wasn't exactly his strong suit. Keeping up with the minutiae of his beloved New England Patriots? Yes. Engineering the path utility lines would take over long distances underground? Also yes. Cooking? Definitely not. The one thing he could really cook was spaghetti Bolognese, and even that was mostly just boiling things since he didn't make his sauce from scratch. He'd also recently learned to make shrimp polenta from a cooking class we took in Italy, but he hadn't made it in the past few weeks and I was afraid it was already slipping out of his repertoire. But regardless of that, tacos were way out of his skill set.

We had already planned on hanging out at my house that night—a whopping two doors down from his own—and when I got there, I could tell that Matt had already been there. The lights were blazing and as soon as I opened the door, I could tell that Matt had the heat cranked up because it was toasty warm.

"Matty! Latte!" I called when they didn't immediately appear to greet me.

No response.

"Matty?" I glanced in the downstairs bedroom and then the living room. "Latte?"

On the kitchen table, I found a note. "Be right

back. Taking Latte for a walk. Love, Matty" Under that was a rough drawing of a man walking a dog, both of them with huge smiles on their faces and a joint thought bubble above their heads showing a smiling woman. He'd drawn arrows and labeled each of the characters. "Matty. Latte. Franny." Just in case I couldn't figure it out on my own.

I smiled and put the note down. Figuring I may as well get comfortable since I didn't know how long they'd been gone, and knowing they took some lengthy walks, even in the cold, I changed into a sweatshirt and some lounge pants, and pulled my hair up into a messy bun. My hair, thick as it was, provided great insulation during our cold Massachusetts winters, but now that I was indoors for the night—and in a comfortably heated space to boot—I wanted it up and out of my way.

I fixed myself an eggnog latte using the fresh batch of eggnog I'd made the night before. Now that I'd discovered how delicious it was, I wasn't ready to give it up just because the holidays were basically over and eggnog was going out of season. I was about to sit down on the couch when I decided to make the house even warmer and cozier by building a fire in the fireplace. When that was done, I sat down on the couch with my latte to wait for Matt and Latte. They had to be back any minute.

But they weren't. Five minutes. Then ten. Then fifteen. Even for them, it was a long walk, especially considering the cold. I had just picked up my phone to call Matt when the door burst open.

"Sorry!" Matt said as Latte bounded over to me, jumping right up on the couch to lick my face. "Apparently lots of people were craving Mexican tonight!"

It was then that I realized he had two big plastic bags in his hands.

"Did you—?" I started before cutting myself off as I tried to process what exactly I was seeing.

"You said you wanted tacos. I got you tacos."

I stared at him blankly.

"Is that okay?"

I fought off Latte's kisses, but down my coffee, walked across the room, took Matt's face in my hands, and kissed him. "You really went out in this weather just to buy me tacos?" I asked when I finally pulled my lips away from his.

He grinned. I kissed him again.

A few minutes later, we had the table covered with the impressive assortment of tacos Matt had picked up.

"I know you get different ones sometimes," he said by way of explanation.

And he had handled it by getting tacos with every different type of meat they had.

I surveyed the spread, then looked at him and smiled. "I love you."

He grinned. "I don't know whether to be

impressed or offended that tacos are all it takes to get an 'I love you' out of you."

"Oh stop," I said, punching his arm lightly. "I already loved you. Tacos just . . . help."

Matt laughed. "Well then, let's eat before they get cold."

We sat and ate. He had been smart enough to get the mini tacos, so I didn't feel bad about helping myself to one of each. Well, at least one.

"How'd it go with the phone list?" Matt asked around a mouthful of carnitas. The night before, I'd told him all about my conversations with Bonnie and Ryan and my plans for calling Cheryl's friends.

I made a face.

"Carne asada not good?"

I shook my head. "No, it's great. That was my reaction to your question."

He looked thoughtful for a second, and then I saw the understanding spread across face. "That good, huh?"

I rolled my eyes. "I got a few people to talk, and a lot of people obviously didn't like her, but nobody seemed like they hated her enough to kill her. Or want her dead. Or be happy that she was dead. Most of the people I talked to sounded like legitimately nice people who had crossed paths with her and were happy to move along."

Matt nodded as he chewed. I took it as an invitation to keep talking.

"It was frustrating, you know? All those phone calls and all I've really learned is that Cheryl was just as crazy as I thought she was." I grabbed one of the chips Matt had brought and dipped it in the salsa. He was still chewing, or chewing again. I wasn't sure. "Or maybe she was a little crazier. Consistently crazy, I guess. This thing with Sammy wasn't a fluke. It wasn't really about Cheryl wanting Ryan back so much. Apparently she was like that with everybody. Even if she broke up with a guy, him moving on made her crazy. It was like she wanted them to be broken-hearted forever."

I munched the chip glumly, then took another. Matt kept working on his taco. Or maybe he'd finished that taco and moved on to the next. I wasn't really sure. All I knew was that he was eating a taco. And Cheryl was crazy. And I didn't have a murder suspect. I stared into the salsa.

"Maybe the roadblock you're running into is the same as the reason that the police haven't found another suspect," he said when he finally finished—or took a break from—chewing.

I looked up at him sharply. "You *cannot* possibly think that Sammy killed Cheryl!"

"What?" He looked genuinely confused. "No! Of course not! Sammy wouldn't kill an ant."

"I think the expression is that she wouldn't kill a fly, but I agree with you either way."

"It doesn't matter what kind of bug she wouldn't

kill. It matters that she wouldn't kill it. And she wouldn't. We know that. What I'm saying is that maybe there's a reason no one—you or the police—has found someone else with a motive for murder. Maybe whoever killed her didn't have one."

I blinked. He resumed eating his taco. "You mean . . . you think it was random?"

He shrugged and kept chewing.

"In Cape Bay?"

Another shrug. More chewing.

"You think there's a random New Year's Eve murderer wandering the streets of Cape Bay?"

He swallowed. "I didn't say it was a well-thought-out theory. Just that it was a theory. Everyone's running around, assuming someone must have hated Cheryl so much they wanted to kill her, but maybe whoever did it didn't even know who Cheryl was. Maybe she was just in the wrong place at the wrong time."

"In Ryan's backyard. On New Year's Eve."

"Well, it's definitely not where she was supposed to be."

"I'll give you that." I resumed staring, at the chips this time, as I mulled the idea over. It was definitely *possible*. In the same way that it was *possible* to have an eighty degree day in the middle of January. Neither one seemed particularly *likely* though. Not in Cape Bay anyway. But it was *possible*.

The other problem with that theory was that I

couldn't exactly investigate *random*. There was no camera footage to review, no way for me to ask the lab to run all the DNA again, no way for me to even know if they'd actually run all the DNA in the first place, or if maybe they'd missed a sample somewhere, somehow. No, unless someone came into Antonia's and casually mentioned that they'd strangled someone in a police officer's backyard on New Year's Eve, there was no way for me to figure out who might have *randomly* killed Cheryl. The only way for me to help Sammy was to double down on investigating Cheryl's life, so I could figure out who wanted her dead. Of course, I wasn't exactly sure how to do that since my phone-a-thon had been fruitless.

"So, what are you going to do?" Matt asked, swallowing down yet another taco. Even for mini tacos, he was really putting them away.

I took a deep breath and let it out slowly. I looked at him across the table and told the truth. "I don't know."

Chapter 15

"I KNOW WHAT TO DO!"

I had woken up the next morning still as indecisive as ever. I took a long, hot shower, took Latte for a long walk, took another long, hot shower to warm back up—all the things you're supposed to do to clear your head, but nothing was working. Maybe a yoga class would work.

The gym's website showed that a class was scheduled to start in about an hour, but there was nothing that said whether there were any spots available, so I picked up my phone, tapped in the gym's number, waited through the excessively long list of options, finally got through to a person, and immediately got put on hold. I had plenty of time, so I waited. And waited. And waited. I was starting to lose my patience when I finally muttered, "I should just go over there and ask in person."

I pulled the phone away from my ear and disconnected the call just as someone came on the line. I didn't care though. Was that it? Was that the answer? Just go there? Was that crazy or did it really make the most sense? I felt like it made the most sense of anything I'd thought of so far.

The phone still in my hand, I dialed Matt's number. As soon as he answered the phone, I blurted it out. "I know what to do!"

"You do? What? What about?" he asked, clearly barely knowing who was on the other end of the line, let alone what I was talking about. He was probably still doing something on his computer and had picked up the phone expecting it to be the receptionist telling him he had a package, but instead it was me, yelling in his ear about my breakthrough.

"I have to go to Plymouth!"

"Plymouth," Matt muttered. "Plymouth? Wait, what? Franny? Why do you have to go to Plymouth?"

"To find out more about Cheryl!"

"But—what? I'm confused. Why do you need to go to Plymouth to find out more about Cheryl?"

"Because that's where she was from!"

Silence.

At that point, I almost wondered if I needed to remind him who Cheryl was. I could hear him murmuring something on the other end of the line, then the keys of his keyboard clicking.

"Okay, sorry," he said, talking to me again. "I had

to get an email off to my boss before she goes into this meeting. So you're going to Plymouth to learn more about Cheryl?"

"Yes, because that's where she and Ryan were from."

This time, I could tell his silence was from him thinking through what I'd said.

"Do you want me to go with you?" he asked finally. "I can't get off this week. I have to get the as-builts for Huntingdon finished up and—"

"You don't need to come. I just wanted to tell you that I figured out what I needed to do."

Another long pause on his end. "Are you sure that's a good idea? Is it safe?"

"It's not like Plymouth is a hotbed of crime."

"No, but that's not really what I meant."

"So what did you mean?"

"I'm just wondering if it's really a good idea for you to go knocking on doors in a strange city looking for a murderer."

I drummed my fingers on the table. Matt was not as excited about this as I'd expected him to be. "Plymouth isn't exactly a strange city, Matty. It's just a little ways up the coast." Saying it out loud made me wonder why I hadn't thought of just driving up there before. It seemed so obvious now.

"I know, but—I don't exactly like the idea of my girlfriend going off all by herself to hunt for a murderer."

I wondered where he'd been the past few months that this was throwing him for a loop. It wasn't the first murder I'd investigated and it wouldn't be the first time I went around by myself asking people for information.

He must have finally realized the same thing. "I know it's not the first time you've done it, but you're usually in town, talking to people who more or less know who you are."

"Are you saying you don't want me to go?"

He paused for a second. "Well, of course I don't want you to go. I like having you around." I could hear the smile in his voice.

"Me being around town while you're at work all day?"

"It's nice knowing you're there. Just in case."

"Just in case of what?"

"In case I leave work early and have a craving for a good cup of coffee made by a pretty girl."

I laughed softly. It was kind of cute hearing how he liked knowing I was around, just in case he wanted to see me. "I appreciate that, but I'm still going to Plymouth."

"I know you are. Will you go up today?"

I hadn't really thought that through yet. Plymouth wasn't far, but I still wanted to have a plan for what I was going to do and who I was going to talk to. "I don't know. I probably need to talk to Ryan again to know where to go, so it'll depend on when I can get a hold of him."

Matt's voice when it came sounded distant, and I realized he was talking to someone in his office. "Sorry, Franny, I have to go," he said, coming back on the line. "My boss needs me in that meeting with her after all. Let me know what you're going to do, okay?"

"I will. I love you."

"Love you too," he said, and the phone clicked off.

I put my phone down on the table and stared at it for a few minutes, trying to decide what I needed to do first. Finally, I got out the spiral-bound notebook Ryan had given me and started making notes about who from the day before I wanted to talk to again. I wasn't sure if I'd get much more information out of them in person than I had on the phone, but I had to try. I knew from many years' experience that it was harder to say no to someone in person than it was on the phone. I also knew it was easier to read people in person, and this was the kind of situation where I needed to know if someone was hiding something. I again shook my head at how long it had taken me to realize I needed to go to Plymouth.

With my list done, I texted Ryan to ask him to meet me at the café in half an hour. Then I texted Sammy that I would be meeting him there and wanted to talk to her too. I had another idea brewing, but I wasn't sure about it yet. I didn't really have any intention of spending the night up in Plymouth, but decided to pack an overnight bag anyway. You never knew what could happen, and it never hurt to be prepared.

The bag packed, I let Latte out and gave him a good belly rub. Then I slipped him one of the special chew toys that had been part of my Christmas present to him. He gave me a big, wet, sloppy kiss of thanks, and I headed out the door to the café. I even drove so that I could leave straight from the café.

I got there during the late morning lull. It was always a nice time. There were a couple of regulars tucked away in corners, typing away on their laptops or curled up with a book and everything was quiet. It would be a good time to have a private conversation.

"Hey!" Sammy called when she saw me. "I got your text. Did you figure something out about the case?"

"Sort of," I replied. I didn't want to tell her quite yet. I wanted to wait for Ryan.

He didn't keep us waiting long. When he strolled in, I was happy to see that he didn't have Mike with him. I'd realized too late that I should have specifically asked him to come alone, but either he'd guessed it on his own or Mike hadn't been around when he left. Probably the latter.

"So what's up, Fran?" he asked. Sammy handed him the eggnog latte she'd already prepared for him, and I caught the sweet smile that passed between them.

"Have a seat. Both of you."

They exchanged a worried glance, but sat down anyway. I sat down too, and put my notebook out in front of me.

"So," I said, speaking quietly. The laptop typer and the reader looked engrossed in what they were doing, but after spending many years working or hanging out in coffee shops, I'd long since realized that people could look busy and still eavesdrop. "I realized that if I'm going to make any headway in this case, I need to go up to Plymouth."

Sammy and Ryan both nodded slightly. I felt even more like it had taken me way too long to realize this is what I should do.

"Ryan." I plowed ahead. "I have a list of people I want to talk to. Some of them, I think I could call, and they'd agree to a meeting. Some of them though —I think I need to just show up. Do you think you can help me figure out where to find them?"

"Do you have the list?" he asked.

I nodded and slid the notebook across to him, turned to the page with the names on it.

He ran his finger down the list, nodding mostly. A couple of times, he looked mildly surprised, but he kept going. I guessed it was the police training that kept him level and cool under unusual circumstances.

It had also come in handy when he showed up half naked while I was standing in his living room.

"Yeah, I can help you," he said after he got to the bottom of the list. "Got a pen?"

I handed it to him and he proceeded to make notes all down the page. When he was done, he pushed it back to me and I scanned through what he'd written. It all worked. It all made sense.

"What else?" he asked.

I asked him a few questions that had come up the day before—how one person knew another, whether they were related or had gone to school together or had dated. I had a few questions, too, about things people had mentioned.

"That it?" he asked when we'd gone through it all.

"There's one more thing," I said slowly.

Ryan cocked an eyebrow.

I looked at Sammy. "I want you to come with me."

Now she raised her eyebrows. "You do? Why? You saw me the other day at Bonnie's—I hardly said a word and then started crying when we left." Ryan put his arm around her supportively.

"I know, but—I don't think it matters if you say anything or not. I think seeing you is what will make the difference. You won't be just some distant person accused of murder—you'll be a real, flesh-and-blood human being who is being accused of something you didn't do. Anyone who has a heart will want to help you."

Sammy looked at Ryan. He shrugged. "I don't know…" she said slowly.

I didn't really want to do it, but I went in for the kill. "What good does it do for you to sit around here and wait for that Dick Phillips to throw the book at you? Why stay here when you can go out and help me solve this?"

She looked pained. "What about the café?"

"I'll ask Rhonda to come in. And if she can't be here, we can close."

Sammy looked shocked.

"I can close the café for a few days or I can lose the person who makes everything run smoothly. Closing the café for a few days seems like a better option."

She looked at Ryan again. "Well… I guess…" she said slowly.

"You guess what?"

"I'll go," she said quietly, staring at the table. Then she looked at me and repeated it, stronger this time. "I'll go. I'll go."

"Good!" I flipped my notebook closed and stood up. "Now you go pack a bag, and I'll call Rhonda."

"Pack a bag? How long are we going to be gone?" she asked.

"However long it takes."

Chapter 16

IN ALL HONESTY, Plymouth wasn't far enough away from Cape Bay that we really needed to spend the night. We could have easily driven back and forth as many times as we needed to. But this was important. Finding out more about Cheryl and who could have wanted her dead was absolutely critical to saving Sammy from going to prison. It needed to be our sole focus right now and parking ourselves in a hotel until we got the information we needed seemed like the way to go.

I had booked a room for us online before we left Cape Bay. It was one of those midlevel hotels where the rooms were clean and reasonably up-to-date, and you got free breakfast. The coffee in those places was usually pretty suspect, but most of the time they had a coffee maker in the room that I could fiddle with until I got it to produce something halfway decent. Just to be on the safe side, I grabbed some of my own fresh-roasted, fresh-ground coffee beans before we left. Just in case whatever was in the room was even worse than what I expected.

I drove us to the hotel first so we could check in and drop off our things. The college-age kid at the desk gave us the speech about the hours breakfast was served, and we headed up to our room on the third floor next to the ice machine. At least if we needed ice, we wouldn't have to go far. The room had two double beds and a view of . . . well, nothing, pretty much. A parking lot and a chain restaurant. But we weren't there for the view anyway. We were there to figure out who killed Cheryl. So that's what we headed out to do.

In addition to the people I knew I wanted to talk to, Ryan had given us the names of a couple more people he'd thought of who might have information on Cheryl. He even contacted some of them himself to let them know we were coming and that we weren't crazy people with some made up excuse to talk to them. Not that it should have been surprising that he did that, of course, since it was his girlfriend that was under investigation.

He arranged for us to meet up with an old friend of his and Cheryl's—Stephanie Lewis—a girl who had been in their circle of friends back in high school. He said that she'd always been close to Cheryl and he thought they still kept in touch. We met her at a chain coffee shop that I wasn't particularly fond of. I wasn't about to complain though. Getting information to get Sammy off the hook was way more important at the moment than subjecting myself to some burnt-tasting coffee.

When we got there, we didn't see anyone who looked like she might be waiting for us, so we headed straight up to the counter to order. I almost got an espresso. I wanted that steaming jolt of caffeine. But then I remembered how bad the last one I'd gotten at this place had been and ended up staring at the menu for five minutes while I let first Sammy and then two other people go in front of me. I finally decided on a white chocolate peppermint mocha. I was pretty sure no burnt coffee flavor could get through that combination of flavors.

By the time I finished ordering, Sammy already had her drink and was sitting at a table in an animated discussion with the woman across from her. I slid into the seat next to Sammy.

"You must be Fran!" the woman said enthusiastically. She stuck her hand out for me to shake. "I'm Stephanie. You look exactly the way Ryan said you would! So does Sammy, actually. I recognized her from his description as soon as I walked in! Good thing, I guess, since he's a cop. It would be pretty bad if he wasn't good at describing people."

I nodded quietly as I shook her hand. I had a feeling I could already tell why Ryan sent us to

Stephanie. She didn't seem like the type of woman to hold much of anything back.

"I better go order my drink," Stephanie said and hopped up to head over to the counter.

"She seems enthusiastic," I said.

"She is," Sammy agreed. "Really nice though."

I nodded and glanced at Sammy's drink as she took a sip. "What'd you get?"

"This?" she asked, looking down at it. "A London Fog tea latte."

Tea. I hadn't thought of that. I knew a little bit about some of the finer points of making a really good cup of tea, but not enough to be picky. Tea would have been perfect.

"Fran!" The voice from the other side of the counter called out. I got up to get my drink and brought it back to the table.

"What about you?" Sammy asked.

I muttered my answer.

"What?"

"A white chocolate peppermint mocha!" I repeated.

Sammy blinked at me a few times. "Are you serious? Are you feeling okay?"

I nodded and took a sip of my drink. It tasted like dessert. A really, really sweet, strong dessert. But not at all like burnt coffee. I tried to keep my expression neutral though because I knew Sammy was watching me.

"How is it?" she asked.

"It's . . . um . . . it's sweet."

Sammy giggled. I knew she actually liked sweet coffee drinks, and I didn't fault her for that. They just weren't my style. At all.

Stephanie bopped back over to our table with her coffee cup. I knew that meant one thing—black coffee.

"You guys both got fancy drinks, didn't you? That makes sense since Ryan said you both work in a coffee shop! I just like it plain so I can really taste the coffee!"

I tried not to visibly cringe. I was all for people who didn't want a bunch of other stuff getting in the way of their being able to really taste the flavor of their coffee. Espresso, an americano, plain drip coffee —they were all fine in my book. The only problem was that I could smell the burnt aroma coming from her cup from all the way across the table. She wanted to be able to really taste her coffee, but what she was tasting wasn't good.

"If you're ever around Cape Bay, you should stop in to Antonia's," I said, as levelly as I could.

Sammy nodded. "If you think that's good, you should taste Fran's coffee."

"Ooh! I will! Cape Bay's down at the beach, right?"

I told her it was and explained where it was in relation to other places she knew, then told her exactly how to find Antonia's if she was ever in town. She seemed interested and I hoped she'd come visit someday, if only so I could show her what good coffee tasted like.

"So, did Ryan tell you why we wanted to talk to you?" I asked after a few minutes of discussing the various little beach towns along the Massachusetts coast.

"He did! That's so crazy what's going on. It's really sad about Cheryl, too. I mean—murdered!" Stephanie said the last word a little louder than I really would have liked her to. Several people around us turned and looked at us like we were discussing something highly questionable. Which we were, so their concerns weren't unfounded.

"Yes," I said, extra quietly in hopes that she'd get the hint. "Especially since the police seem to be having trouble coming up with any suspects other than Sammy here. And everyone who knows Sammy knows she'd never kill anyone. I've seen her scoop a spider up and take it outside instead of killing it." I snuck a look at Sammy and saw her staring at the table, a slight flush on her cheeks. I wondered whether she was uncomfortable talking about the case or hearing for the umpteenth time how she'd never hurt a fly. Or maybe it was just the warmth of the coffee shop. It *was* getting a little warm in there.

I looked back at Stephanie. "I can't let Sammy go to jail just because the police officer investigating won't investigate anyone other than Sammy, so I'm looking for other suspects myself." I lowered my voice another notch. "Do you know anyone who could have wanted Cheryl dead?"

Stephanie laughed.

I stared. That wasn't the reaction I'd expected.

"Sorry! For laughing, I mean." She regained her composure. "It's just that, well, yeah! I can think of quite a few people."

I blinked a few times. The police could only come up with Sammy, but Stephanie could think of *quite a few* people?

"I know that sounds crazy! Saying they wanted her dead might be a little strong, but—Cheryl was a homewrecker. I mean, I don't know if anyone ever actually got divorced because of her, but she sure caused some breakups. A *lot* of breakups. It was kind of ridiculous, really."

"How so?" I had an idea, but I wanted to hear what she had to say.

"She never let anybody go! Well, she did—it wasn't like she was in a lot of long-term relationships." Stephanie laughed at that. "She just changed her mind a lot. A *lot!*"

"So she would go back to her exes?" I noticed out of the corner of my eye that Sammy seemed to be listening intently.

Stephanie nodded and took a sip of her terrible coffee. "She'd at least try! I don't think she liked seeing people move on—at all! I know some guys broke it off with their new girlfriends because they wanted to get back with Cheryl—some of the girls broke it off though because they couldn't take Cheryl's meddling!"

Sammy stared out the window. I wondered if she'd thought about breaking up with Ryan just to get rid of Cheryl and her constant, creepy text messages.

"So you think one of them might have been mad enough at Cheryl for ruining their relationship that they followed her to Cape Bay and killed her?" Saying it out loud made it sound pretty crazy, but then again, it was also pretty crazy of Cheryl to follow Ryan to Cape Bay and harass his new girlfriend.

Stephanie shrugged. "I mean, I guess it could happen, right? If someone was upset enough?"

"Do you know who might have been upset enough?"

Stephanie leaned in. "Honestly?"

I waited in anticipation. With any luck, she'd give us the name of a person who, when we went to talk to them, would take one look at Sammy and confess. Then they'd come back to Cape Bay with us and make their confession to that awful Dick Phillips who would immediately drop the case against Sammy and arrest that person. Okay, that exact scenario was unlikely, but I was hopeful that Stephanie was about to give us the single piece of information that would break the case wide open.

"Honestly, I don't really know."

I felt like someone stuck a pin in me. I felt deflated.

"Cheryl was so toxic, I pretty much stopped hanging out with her a while ago. A lot of people did. I don't really know who her latest conquests were."

I took a long drink from my sickly sweet drink and wished it were something stronger, like straight espresso. Or whiskey.

"I know that's not what you wanted to hear, but I've just really been avoiding her!"

I sighed. "Do you know anyone who hasn't been avoiding her?"

"Just a couple people!" She rattled off their names and I jotted them down on a napkin. One of them was a name Ryan had given us, but the other one was new to me. "I'm sorry! I know that's probably not very helpful!"

"That's okay," I said, not really feeling it. "You gave us some information that we can work with. We appreciate that. Thank you."

We mumbled some more pleasantries, but I didn't really feel much like chatting. I was disheartened, but at the same time, I wanted to get a move on and try to talk to some more people. After a few more minutes, we put our coats on, Stephanie got her bad coffee topped off, and we headed out. Stephanie gave us directions to the next place we were going. Just before

I got in the car, a thought crossed my mind. "Hey Stephanie? One more question."

"Sure!"

"Can you think of any particularly nasty breakups Cheryl was a part of? Even if they were a long time ago?"

She thought for a minute. "Chris Miller! That one was bad—really bad. And it wasn't even that long ago."

A car in the parking lot honked. When I looked over, the driver made a gesture to indicate that he was waiting for my parking spot and was getting impatient that I wasn't leaving yet. I thought about gesturing back, but decided it probably wasn't a good idea. I turned back to Stephanie. "Chris Miller?"

"Yes! It was messy. I think they were engaged!"

The driver behind me revved his engine. I thought about going back into the coffee shop and getting another cup, but, well, that probably wasn't a good idea either. If I deliberately provoked him, he would probably turn out to be someone critical to the case. Besides, it wasn't nice.

"Thanks!" I called back to Stephanie and slipped into the car. I put the car into reverse and asked Sammy to text Ryan to ask about Chris Miller. I wasn't sure, but I had a feeling Stephanie had just given us our first solid lead.

Chapter 17

WE SPENT the rest of the day talking to people that Ryan and Cheryl knew, either now or back when they were in high school, before Ryan moved away. The picture they painted of Cheryl was remarkably consistent—she had trouble getting over men, she was addicted to men and being in a relationship. She was an extreme version of the stereotype of someone who can't—or can't stand to—be single. She moved from relationship to relationship, constantly dating someone or other.

From what they said, "serial monogamist" wasn't quite the right phrase to describe her. Maybe "serial romantic." From what they said, she was a grass-is-always-greener type—if she wasn't happy in *this* relationship, maybe she would be in *that* one. Or if *that* one hadn't worked out, maybe it was a matter of timing. It sounded like she never really fell out of love with anyone—just fell more in love with someone else. I was surprised to find myself feeling almost sympathetic towards her. It sounded like she wasn't really crazy, just . . . lost. Especially when it came to Ryan.

Her friends—and former friends—almost all mentioned that Ryan was, in Cheryl's opinion, the one who got away. They said that him moving away made it easier for her to idealize him. She became obsessed with stories of high school sweethearts who got back together many years later and lived happily ever after. And when he moved back to Massachusetts over the summer, well, that just meant they really were meant to be after all.

Some of her close friends surprised me by agreeing to talk to us—I guessed because I was trying to figure out who killed her, after all. They wanted her murderer punished, too. Unsurprisingly, they were even more sympathetic towards her. They knew she had her flaws, but they loved her anyway. Of course, when I remembered the crazy text messages she'd sent and what she did to Sammy's apartment, I felt a little less forgiving.

The thing that surprised me the most from everyone we talked to was that, according to them, aside from her romantic obsessions, Cheryl was otherwise completely normal. She was a good friend. She was funny. She loved kids and did volunteer work with underprivileged children. She was just crazy when it came to romance.

We still had a couple of people to talk to. We were going to have breakfast in the morning with Chris Miller, the guy Stephanie had mentioned. A couple of the other people we had spoken to during the day mentioned him as well. Whatever had happened with him had only been a few months earlier, so it was fresh in everyone's minds. Based on that, I was actually surprised that he agreed to talk to us, but he had. Of course, he still had time to back out, but I hoped he didn't. I thought it was strange that no one suggested that we talk to his ex-girlfriend, but the way they talked about her made it seem like she was unavailable, like she'd moved out of town or something.

The other person I really wanted to talk to was Cheryl's mom. Cheryl's friends had brought up more than once how contentious Cheryl's relationship with her mother was. Apparently they'd never gotten along, but things got worse when Cheryl was old enough to start dating. Her friends thought Cheryl's mother viewed her as competition even though, to their knowledge, Cheryl preferred to stick to men her own age.

All of that was what I thought about as I got ready for bed that night in the hotel bathroom. It had been a long day, and my head was swimming with all the information we'd learned. I was frustrated that no one had turned out to be an obvious murder suspect, but I reminded myself that it had never been likely that we'd talk to someone who would volunteer that they had killed Cheryl. In fact, most of them seemed sad about Cheryl's death. That was, I supposed, a good thing in the greater scheme of things, but at the moment what I really wanted to find was someone who wasn't sad about it at all. I wanted to find someone who was happy, and maybe a little proud, that she was dead. And so far, I hadn't. I'd even asked everyone, just casually, what they'd done on New Year's Eve in the hopes that I would trip someone up, but it didn't work. And since most of them were friends, they were almost all at the same parties that basically gave them the same alibis. I had to put my hopes in Chris Miller and Cheryl's mom. At the very least, I hoped they would give me another lead to follow up on.

I dabbed my moisturizer on my face, ran a brush through my thick mane of black hair, and left the bathroom. When I'd gone in, Sammy had just gotten on the phone with Ryan, so I'd taken my time to give them some privacy. When I came out, at first I thought they were still on the phone. Sammy was sitting on the edge of her bed, facing away from me with her head down, her long blonde hair cascading around her shoulders. She didn't often wear it down, so I was distracted for a few seconds by how long it really was. Then, I noticed that her hair was shaking —and her shoulders underneath it were, too. She was crying.

"Sammy?" I said quietly, afraid to startle her even though she must have heard the bathroom door open. "Sam, are you okay?" It was a silly question since she clearly wasn't, but it's what came out.

"Fran, I—" She broke off into more vigorous sobs.

I dropped my toiletry bag on the bed and went over to kneel in front of her. "What's wrong?" I asked. "What happened? Did Ryan say something on the phone, or—?" I didn't know what else it could be, other than that she was a murder suspect, of course, so I just let my voice trail off.

Sammy nodded. Her face was in her hands, so it was a whole body movement.

"What did he say?"

She tried to take a breath, but it came out as a sob. She tried again, but it was another sob. Finally, she managed to speak. "The police searched my apartment."

I sat in confusion for a few seconds. "Didn't you want them to do that? To see what Cheryl did?" I could, of course, see how it could still be upsetting, but I was hoping that reminder would help calm her, at least a little.

She nodded her full-body nod again. "But that's not why they searched it. Ryan said Detective Phillips didn't believe that wasn't how I keep the apartment. And—and—he said that Cheryl's fingerprints being in there didn't prove that I wasn't there when she came. He thinks I invited her there. That we were friends or something! And I got jealous! He thinks I faked all those texts somehow and I got jealous of her relationship with Ryan and killed her over it. But what relationship? They didn't have one anymore. He didn't even know she was still in town. Fran, he's made up this whole story to explain how I killed her and why, but none of it's true. The whole thing's made up. And I'm going to go to jail because of it."

I sat back on my heels. That was not what I had expected would happen when they searched the apartment. It had seemed so obvious when I was there. Because I knew Sammy. Which Phillips didn't.

"That's not even the worst of it," she said quietly.

I looked up at her abruptly. Her face was still covered by her hands, but she seemed to have mostly stopped crying.

"It's not?" I asked, getting a distinctly nauseated feeling in my stomach.

She shook her head and I could hear her suck in a long, slow breath.

"What else did he say?"

"They've been questioning people."

"Other suspects? That's great—"

"No. My family. My friends. They called Dawn in today. And my mom. My mom, Fran!"

"Oh wow. Wow."

"They put Ryan on leave. They told him not to come back until this case was resolved."

"Oh my gosh."

"If I go to jail, he's going to lose his job?"

"Did he say that?" I asked.

"He didn't have to. How are they going to keep a police officer on the force whose girlfriend is in jail for murdering his ex-girlfriend in his backyard?"

When she put it that way, I could see her point.

"They're going to arrest me, Fran."

My nurturing streak kicked in. "Now, Sammy, you don't know that. Maybe Dawn and your mom convinced Phillips that you're not that kind of person. Maybe there's some evidence from the search that will show them that you didn't do it. Maybe—"

"Phillips told him."

"Told who what?" I asked, not sure I wanted to know.

"Told Ryan that he's going to arrest me."

I felt like the wind had been knocked out of me. "When?" I whispered.

"Soon. That's all he said. Soon." At that, she started to cry again.

I sat on the floor and put my head in my hands. This was bad. Very bad. I was failing at finding Cheryl's murderer. I was letting Sammy down. I'd come up to Plymouth in an attempt to find the missing pieces, and what had I found? That Cheryl had ruined a lot of relationships. But I wasn't any closer to a solution than I'd been that morning. And what was worse was that I may have wasted some of

Sammy's last days of freedom doing it. Days that she could have spent with Ryan, with Dawn, with her mom. Days she could have spent on the beach, feeling the wind in her hair and the sand between her toes. Okay, in early January she probably wouldn't have been walking barefoot on the beach, at least not for long, but she could have if she'd wanted to—if I hadn't dragged her to Plymouth with me.

Of course, I knew that as bad as I felt, Sammy felt worse. After all, it was her life on the line. But it wasn't over yet. She hadn't been arrested, tried, or convicted. She was still a free woman, and that meant I still had a chance to redeem myself—and save her. I hoped that Chris Miller or Cheryl's mother would have the answers I was looking for, but if they didn't, I would just have to find someone else who did.

Chapter 18

NEITHER OF US slept well that night. I tossed and turned and was in and out of bed what felt like a dozen times. I could hear Sammy sniffling off and on in her bed, which just made my anxiety higher. She didn't deserve this. No one did, but of everyone I knew, Sammy was the one who least deserved the anguish of being falsely accused of murder. And, of course, she was the one who would feel it the most.

I drifted off once or twice, but was jolted awake every time by nightmares about Sammy being arrested. Then it would take forever for me to calm down and get the images of her being hauled off to jail out of my head. Then I would go to the bathroom. Then I would hear Sammy crying. Then I would start to drift off again, only for some version of the cycle to start all over again. By the time I saw the crack of light reach through the slight gap in our hotel room's blackout shades, I was thrilled to finally be able to reasonably get up and out of bed.

I took a long, hot shower and got myself dressed. When I came out of the bathroom, Sammy was sitting on the edge of her bed, just like she had the night before. My heart lurched in my chest as a wave of fear that she'd had more bad news crashed over me.

"Sammy?" I said quietly.

"Morning, Fran," she replied with a yawn and a big stretch. She turned around, rubbing her eyes. "I think I'd just fallen asleep when my alarm went off. Hopefully you got more sleep than I did."

I breathed a sigh of relief that she was just having trouble waking up. I wasn't sure either of us could have handled more bad news. "I guess you didn't hear me tossing and turning all night."

"I was too busy tossing and turning myself." She yawned again.

We had apparently switched places for the day—usually I was the one reluctantly dragging myself out of bed at the last possible moment, and she was the early bird, getting to the café at the crack of dawn to open it up and greet the morning regulars I only vaguely knew existed. Of course I would have liked to still be in bed, sleeping peacefully, but since that hadn't been what I was doing, being up and about would do just fine for the day.

While Sammy got dressed and ready to go, I

called Matt. I tried to hide how stressed I was feeling, but he could hear it in my voice.

"What's going on, Franny? What's wrong?" he asked almost immediately.

I almost broke down into tears, but managed to fight them back. "If we don't figure out who really killed Cheryl, Sammy's going to be arrested," I said quietly into the phone, trying to keep my voice from carrying into the bathroom.

"You knew that before you went up there, didn't you?" asked Matt, ever the logical engineer. "That was the whole reason you started investigating."

"Yes, but yesterday Ryan heard the detective say he was going to do it soon. Right before they sent Ryan home on leave."

"Oh. Well, yeah, that's bad." A distinctive panting noise came from his end of the phone.

"Is that Latte?" I asked, even though he would have to be cheating on me with another dog for the source of the noise to be anything else.

"Sure is. You want to talk to him?"

I did and proceeded to make assorted embarrassing baby talk noises into the phone for a minute or two. But I didn't care. Because as much as I missed Matt, I may have missed Latte a little more. I would have given almost anything to curl up on the couch and have his warm body pressed against me. With an occasional face lick for good measure. Dogs were so comforting.

After Latte wandered away to go chew a bone or something, I talked to Matt for a few more minutes until Sammy came out of the bathroom. Then she and I packed up our things and checked out of the hotel. If we weren't back in Cape Bay tonight, we'd be in Boston, since that's where Cheryl's mom apparently was.

We went to the restaurant where we were supposed to meet Chris Miller for breakfast. I took a risk and ordered a cup of coffee which turned out to be surprisingly good.

Chris showed up about ten minutes after we arrived—just long enough for me to have gotten anxious that he wasn't going to come at all. I was actually stewing over that possibility when he walked up.

"You must be Fran and Sammy," he said, sliding quickly into the booth, but not so quickly that I missed seeing that he was rather on the short side. "I'm Chris. You guys wanted to talk to me about Cheryl?"

"We heard from a few of your friends that you had a bad breakup recently that Cheryl was somehow involved in. Would you mind telling us about that?" I asked.

He eyeballed us warily. "You guys cops?"

"No," Sammy and I said together. I hoped it didn't sound like something we'd rehearsed.

"The police are actually set on Sammy being the

prime suspect, so we're trying to find out who the actual murderer was so she doesn't go to jail."

Chris laughed. "That's crazy. Did you ever think that maybe it was just random? People get killed for being in the wrong place at the wrong time sometimes, you know."

"Not in Cape Bay they don't," I replied coldly. It wasn't a lie. Cape Bay had had more than its fair share of murders over the past few months, but none of them were because someone was in the wrong place at the wrong time.

"So you two think you can figure it out when the cops can't?"

"The detective on the case is from out of town and hasn't ever tried to find a suspect other than Sammy. So, yeah, I think that since we're actually trying, maybe we can find another suspect."

Chris scoffed. "And what if the detective's not wrong? What if Sammy actually killed her?" He looked defiantly across the table at us.

"I didn't kill her," Sammy surprised me by saying. She'd been mostly very quiet when we talked to people. I didn't mind, because she was really just there to put an innocent face to the false accusations, so people could see the person who was about to take the fall for something she didn't do. But now her voice was icy cold, and I could hear in it that she'd had enough of Chris' arguments.

"That's exactly what a murderer would say."

"Or an innocent person——" I started, but Sammy cut me off.

"That's enough! Are you going to talk to us about Cheryl or not? Because if you're not, I'm leaving!"

"Blondie's got some spunk!" Chris grinned.

Sammy stood up. "Come on, Fran. This is a waste of our time." She turned and started walking away. I stood to follow her.

"Wait!" Chris called.

Sammy stopped walking, but didn't turn around.

"How do I know you're not just trying to pin this on me?"

Sammy turned around slowly. "Now *that's* exactly what a murderer would say. Every single other person we've talked to has been more than happy to help us. Because they're normal people who don't want to see an innocent person go to jail. You're the *only* one who has given us grief, and you know what? That makes you look guilty." She turned back around. "Come on, Fran."

"Okay! I'll talk to you!"

I hesitated and looked at Sammy. She looked back at me and shrugged. "It's up to you. But if he starts this up again, I'm leaving."

I looked at Chris.

"I'll be cool. I swear." He held up his hands in surrender.

"You have one chance," I said.

"I got it."

I looked at Sammy. She sighed and came back to the table. We sat down. "Okay, talk," I said.

"Can't we order our food first? I'm starving."

I started to get up.

"Okay, okay! What do you want to know?"

"Tell us about this breakup that Cheryl was involved in."

"It was over the summer—" Chris started.

As if on cue, the waitress walked up. "Sorry about the wait, folks! Are you all ready to order?"

I clenched my jaw in annoyance. Sammy fidgeted next to me like she was seriously considering getting up. Chris didn't even seem fazed.

"Do you guys still have eggnog?" he asked. He drummed on the menu with his fingers, and I noticed that his hands were nearly as small as mine. Small man, small hands. It made sense.

"Nope, sorry, we're all out for the season."

"That's too bad. You guys make the best eggnog." He flinched. "No, my ex made the best eggnog. But yours is a close second." He stared down at his menu. All his bravado faded. As much as he had annoyed me, I could see the pain on his face and felt sympathetic, so I went ahead and ordered my food so he could have a minute. By the time Sammy had ordered, he seemed to have collected himself and was ready to talk again.

"Sorry about that," he said. "My ex is just a sensitive subject for me. Everything still reminds me of her."

I wondered if he'd been argumentative earlier because he wanted to avoid talking about her. "That's okay. I understand it's a painful subject." Sammy scoffed beside me, clearly not having it. I elbowed her and gave her a look. No matter how annoyed she or I might be with him at the moment, we needed him, and so we needed to be nice.

"I thought I was going to marry her," he said, staring at his hands. "We'd talked about it, and I was looking at rings."

"Cheryl?"

Now it was his turn to scoff. "Cheryl? No. Not in a million years. Cheryl wasn't marriage material."

"But you broke up with your ex for her?"

He nodded. "We'd dated a couple of years back and broke up when she started seeing some other guy. She came back around and started calling me again. We hung out a couple of times, flirted and stuff. She was fun, you know?" He looked up at me for approval, and I nodded sympathetically, even though if Matt tried to pull something like that, I'd be furious. "Bea started to get mad about how much time I was spending with Cheryl. She was acting jealous and I started to think that maybe I didn't want to get married after all. I mean, would I rather sit around and play house with Bea judging my every move or go out and party with Cheryl? Bea had turned into a downer. Cheryl was fun." He sighed heavily. "I was hanging out with Cheryl a lot. I missed a date with Bea, and she got really mad. We got in a huge fight about it, and I took off. I ended up at Cheryl's place."

Chris looked at me like he was waiting for my judgement. I bit my tongue to keep from saying anything. Nothing that I could say right now would help us find the person who really killed Cheryl. Besides, I didn't have to say it. He already knew. He looked back down at the table.

"Bea called me in the morning to apologize, but I was in the bathroom. Cheryl answered my phone. By the time I got back to our place, all my stuff was out on the front step. Bea wouldn't even talk to me. Not that I deserved it. I cheated on her. With Cheryl of all people." He looked at me again, and I could see the pain in his eyes. "The guy Bea dated before me broke up with her for Cheryl too."

I tried to keep the shock off my face, but I couldn't. Chris saw it.

"Yeah. I'm a jerk. I knew why she was acting that way about Cheryl, but I didn't care. I was having fun, and I didn't care who I hurt. I'm a jerk."

"Yes, you are," Sammy said before I could stop her.

I thought Chris was going to get mad, leave maybe. But he nodded. "Cheryl didn't even stick around. It lasted maybe a two, three weeks after that, and then she kicked me out for some other guy. I ruined the best relationship I've ever had for something that didn't even last a month."

We sat in silence except for a polite "thank you" while the waitress brought our food. Chris stared at his. I poked at mine. Sammy dug in. She was normally so kind, so sympathetic, with a heart as big as her smile, but Chris' story didn't even faze her. I knew she thought he deserved everything he got.

I poked again at my scrambled eggs. And then, against my better judgement, I was nice to him. "Have you thought about telling Bea how sorry you are? Explain that you know you messed up and beg her to forgive you?"

Sammy looked at me wide-eyed like I was betraying the sisterhood. I was, but I could see how pained Chris was by the whole thing. And I hadn't endured weeks of harassing text messages from Cheryl, so I had a little more distance from the situation.

"I can't," Chris said. "She's gone."

"Gone?" I repeated as tears welled up in his eyes.

He nodded. "It was too much for her. She couldn't take it and she—she's gone."

I wanted to be sick. Instead, I stumbled my way through the handful of questions I still had—where was he on New Year's Eve? (home alone) Did he know where Cape Bay was? (yes, he'd been there several times, once with Bea)—and got us out of there as fast as I could.

"Did he say she—she killed herself?" I asked Sammy once we were safely inside the car.

"I think so," Sammy replied. She'd been shaken, too, when he said it. She'd put her fork down and hadn't touched another bite.

I clenched the steering wheel until my knuckles turned white. "You know," I said carefully. "If you weren't the prime suspect, I don't think I'd care about who killed Cheryl at all."

Chapter 19

THE DRIVE UP to Boston took three times as long as it should have because the traffic was somehow even worse than usual. We were stopped dead on the highway for forty-five minutes for some reason that I could never quite figure out.

Sammy and I were mostly quiet on the trip except for when I needed her to give me directions. Other than that, we were each lost in our own thoughts about the case.

"Are you sure this is it?" I asked as I pulled up in front of a converted townhouse in a sketchy part of Dorchester.

Sammy checked the address on the building and on the paper she held in her hand. "Yup, this is it."

I gave the building another wary look, then sighed and circled the block in search of a parking spot. Once I found one and wedged my car into a too-small parallel parking spot with Sammy's help, I got out and hit the lock button on the keyless entry until the car honked at me. Then I checked the doors. Then I hit the button again, crossed my fingers and said a little prayer that my car and all its contents would still be there when we got back. Sammy and I walked the block and a half back to Cheryl's mother's building.

"You ready?" I asked as I eyed the building once again.

"As much as I'll ever be," Sammy replied.

I at least had the benefit of having lived in New York City for a few years. Sammy had lived her whole life in Cape Bay where locking your doors when you left home was an anomaly and people routinely stored their car keys in the ignition.

I led the way up the steps to the building. There was no buzzer, so we walked right in. I glanced at Sammy.

"2A, right?"

Sammy looked at her paper again and nodded. We climbed to the second floor. I knocked on the first door. We waited. I knocked again. We waited some more.

"She knows we're coming, right?" Sammy asked.

"I told her we were." I was getting a little anxious standing there in the hallway. I'd seen the neighborhood, after all. "Maybe I should just call her." Sammy agreed, so I pulled my phone out and scrolled to find Cheryl's mother in my call history. I found it and tapped the button to call her again. "It's ringing," I whispered.

Sammy shuffled slightly closer to the door. "I can hear it ringing inside, too."

I counted the number of rings on my end. Three, four, five. I was starting to wonder what I would do if she didn't answer. Her phone was clearly inside. What if she was incapacitated? I couldn't in good conscience just leave her there. But maybe she'd forgotten we were coming and gone out, forgetting her phone, too. Maybe she'd just changed her mind about talking to us. The phone was on its sixth ring. I was going to have to decide soon.

"Hello?" I breathed a sigh of relief as a craggy voice finally came through the line.

"Hi Lois!" I said cheerily. "This is Fran Amaro, I spoke with you yesterday about coming to talk to you about your daughter Cheryl. I'm standing outside your apartment right now. I knocked, but there was no answer."

There was a long enough pause that I actually pulled the phone away from my head to look and see if the call was still connected.

"Oh, is that who's out there making all that racket? Hold on, I'll come let you in."

This time I knew the call was disconnected. "She's coming," I told Sammy.

We waited.

After almost a minute, Sammy leaned towards the

door again and listened. "I can hear someone moving around in there."

I wondered if we were at the wrong apartment building after all and if the ringing phone was just a coincidence.

Finally, the door opened. A wall of cigarette smoke hit us and I had to stop myself from involuntarily taking a step backwards to avoid it. "C'mon in," Lois said, a lit cigarette dangling from her lips. Her voice sounded even craggier than it had on the phone.

"We were starting to wonder if we had the wrong apartment!" I said with as much cheerfulness as I could muster.

"I had to go to the can." She led us into the smoky apartment. Sammy coughed quietly behind me. Lois took a seat in an armchair across from the TV showing a group of overly made up, bickering housewives. "Sit down."

Sammy and I sat down on the couch. Well, perched on the edge of it. It was covered with clothes and magazines and empty fast food containers, so the edge was about as far onto it as we could get, even if we'd wanted to sit back further.

The only light in the room was from a single uncovered window—and the TV, of course. In the dim light, you could see the clouds of cigarette smoke wafting through the room.

"So, Lois—" I started.

"Shhhh," she hissed. "I wanna see this."

I turned to look at the TV, at the angry heavily made up women on the screen. I wasn't sure what was going on, but one was crying, with big, black rivers of mascara tears running down her cheeks. Another one was in her face, wagging her finger and yelling about something. After a few minutes, it went to commercial.

"Now, whaddaya want?" Lois rasped without turning away from the laundry detergent commercial now on the screen.

"We were hoping to talk to you about Cheryl. Your daughter."

She scoffed. "Yeah, I know who Cheryl is. Trust me, I don't get confused about somebody who started screwin' up my life before I was even out of high school."

"You were in high school when Cheryl was born?" I did some quick math and realized that meant Lois was barely ten years older than me. Until that moment, I honestly thought she was closer to sixty-five than forty-five.

"Yeah, senior year. I had to drop out and it went downhill from there. The night I got knocked up was the last good night of my life." She took a long drag on her cigarette. "No, I take that back. I went to a really good party a couple of weeks later. *That* was the last good night of my life."

"I'm, uh, I—" I stammered as I tried to come up with the right thing to say in response. "Um, I'm sorry to hear that," I finally managed. "Was Cheryl a difficult child growing up?"

"Shh!" Lois pointed at the TV screen, now showing some of the same women lounging around a pool situated in the backyard of what appeared to be a massive house.

Sammy and I were politely quiet. I stared in the direction of the TV screen, not really watching the show, but not really able to look away from it either. The women were just so over-the-top and so melodramatic. A few minutes later, it went back to commercial.

"So was Cheryl a difficult child growing up?" I asked quickly, realizing that all the talking we did was going to have to be during the commercial breaks.

"You better believe it. So demanding. Always wanting something or other. A real pain in the you-know-what. I had to work two jobs to pay for a place to live and all the food she wanted to stuff in her fat little face all the time. I couldn't ever go out and party with my friends. Not until she got a little older and could stay home by herself for a while." Her cigarette was burning low. She got a fresh one out of the pack and lit it off the end of the one she was smoking. I'd heard of people doing that, but had never actually seen it in person. It was fascinating.

"Some of her friends told me you two haven't been getting along lately?"

Lois snorted. "Lately? Try the past twenty-eight

years. Cheryl's been out to ruin my life since the day she was born."

"How so?"

Lois didn't even shush me this time, just turned back to the TV.

I glanced at Sammy. She looked back at me with wide eyes. Both of our families had our quirks, but nothing like this.

The women on TV continued to argue over something or other. Either one of their husbands or sons, but I couldn't really tell which, just that Braxton was stressing them all out. The one thing I was grateful for was that the show had a *lot* of commercials. I repeated my last question as soon as the next one came on.

"Constant whining and meddling. She always wanted attention. I thought it'd be easier once she got older, but it was worse. Little brat started doin' up her hair and makeup, wearing shirts that barely covered anything around my boyfriends. You try to compete with a sixteen year old when you're a saggy old thirty-four year old."

Being thirty-four, I tried not to take her comment personally, but I'd never actually thought of myself as either saggy *or* old. I actually thought I looked pretty good, especially since I'd taken up kickboxing a few months earlier. Aside from that, I had definitely never considered a sixteen year old competition. And I would have run far, far away from any man that did. After I reported him to the police.

"And you can't get 'er back for somethin' like that neither. What am I gonna do? Steal one of her boyfriends for every one of mine she steals? Like I said, you can't compete with that. That's why I moved up here. She can't steal a man she doesn't know I have."

"So you hadn't talked to Cheryl much lately?"

"Not until she came up here lookin' for money right after Christmas. Said she had to go someplace and needed money for a hotel."

"Did you give it to her?"

Lois looked at me like I'd lost my mind, or maybe never really had one in the first place. "You kiddin'? Heck no, I'm not giving her any of my disability money. I work for that!"

I chose to ignore the obvious irony of her "working" for her disability money.

"She stole some though."

"She did?" I asked, although from what I knew of Cheryl, I wasn't particularly surprised.

"Yep. Two hundred dollars outta my coffee can. I was gonna have to find a new hiding spot, but now I guess I don't have to!" Lois cackled before breaking into a raspy smoker's cough.

The fighting women came back on TV, so I knew I had a couple of minutes to think about what to ask her next. I was ready when the commercial came back.

"So I guess you were pretty upset about Cheryl taking your two hundred dollars."

"Course I was. You know how much cigarettes cost these days? It's like armed robbery going into the smoke shop!"

I changed course. "Do you know where Cape Bay is?"

"You mean that little town down on the Cape? We used to go there all the time when I was a kid. Stayed in a real nice place called the Surfside Inn. I loved it there." She looked nostalgic for a minute as she took a long drag from her cigarette. "Isn't that where Cheryl got killed?"

"Yes, it is," I said, wondering if this was the first time she'd put together that the place she used to go on vacation as a child was the same as the place where her daughter was murdered.

"Figures. I never got to go down there after I got preggers. Ma and Pop cut me off. Kinda poetic justice that that's where Cheryl got knocked off, huh?" She grinned a wide, yellow-toothed smile. I felt a shiver go down my spine. I was ready to wrap this conversation up, but I had one more question I had to ask and Lois' show was back on.

By the time the commercials came back, I had a plan to accomplish both. "I guess that's about it for us!" I said, scooting even further towards the end of the couch. I was now basically hovering over empty space, but the pain in my thighs was worth the quick escape. "It was nice meeting you. Oh, hey, did you get to do anything fun for New Year's Eve?"

Lois eyed me, then grinned again. "You thinkin' I killed 'er? Hate to burst your bubble, but I didn't. I was here with my man. Drank a fifth of whisky each." Her volume suddenly increased. "Didn't we, Joe?"

I almost fell from my awkward squatting position when a man's voice came from the bedroom. I'd had no idea anyone else was in the apartment. "What? You talkin' to somebody, Lo? Somebody here?"

"Yeah, those girls from down the Cape! Come to ask about Cheryl. I told you they was comin'!"

"Cheryl? Who's Cheryl?" The man I had to assume was Joe stumbled out of the bedroom and leaned on the doorframe. He scratched his head and then his gut. I did my best to avoid looking at his gaping boxers which, aside from his socks, were the only articles of clothing on his body.

"I told you! She's my kid who got killed!"

"Oh, right." He scratched his head again. "You got any more smokes?"

"Not for you! All the ones I got left are mine. You gotta go get some of your own. And I only got half a pack left, so we need to go get some more before I run out too."

Joe snorted and muttered something nasty under his breath, then disappeared back into the bedroom.

I stood up. Sammy quickly followed. "Well, I guess we'd better get going so you can get to the store. It was a pleasure to meet you." I reached out to shake Lois' hand, but it was occupied lighting another cigarette. I dropped my hand back by my side. "You have my number if you think of anything else."

She waved her hand in our general direction. Her show was back on.

"We'll let ourselves out," I said and began to move towards the door. Lois grunted. Sammy and I left the apartment and made a beeline back to my car which, fortunately, was still there. We got in, and I pulled out of the parking spot as quickly as I could, getting us on the road back to Cape Bay. I still wasn't sure I knew who killed Cheryl, but I knew that I had one more suspect.

Chapter 20

SOMEWHERE ALONG THE road from Boston to Cape Bay, I noticed Sammy sniffing her coat. She wiggled it off and sniffed her the arm of her sweater. Then she leaned over and sniffed me.

"What are you doing?" I asked.

"We both smell like ashtrays. Very old ashtrays."

Suddenly I smelled it. I'd been so focused on navigating the chaotic Boston streets and then thinking about the case that I hadn't even noticed it until then. But it was bad. Really bad. Not sure these clothes will ever smell right again kind of bad.

"Wow, that's—that's bad," I said.

"How much further is it?" Sammy asked.

"Almost an hour."

"Ugh." Sammy sniffed her arm again.

"We could stop at a gas station and get some air fresheners."

"I don't think that would help. The smell is on me." She sniffed her hand and then held it in front of me.

I swatted her away and sniffed my own hand instead. "Oh gross," I said, realizing that the stale smoke smell really did seem to have seeped into my pores.

"Should we roll down the windows?"

"It's freezing out there!"

"It stinks in here!"

"Wait, I have an idea." I cracked the rear windows open, just enough that I could start to feel the icy outside air blowing on my neck. Then I cranked the heat up as high as it would go. "How's that?"

"The heat makes the smoke smell worse," Sammy said.

"Okay." I turned the heat off.

"But now I'm freezing!"

"Make up your mind!"

"Leave it off! I'd rather freeze and let it air out than choke on the smell."

About five minutes later, I noticed Sammy's hand creep over and turn the heat back on. The smell was bad, but at least we were warm. A few minutes later, she turned it back off. A few minutes after that, she turned it back on. For the rest of the trip, we alternated the heat on and off, each time leaving it until we were too cold or the smell was too bad. Surprisingly, we didn't talk about the case. The constant changing of the temperatures was enough to mostly keep us occupied. My mind did drift in that direction a few times, but mostly I stayed focused on the road, the smell, and the ever-fluctuating temperature.

It was dark by the time I dropped Sammy off at Ryan's. "Still don't want to go home, huh?"

"No, I—" She shook her head like she was shaking off cobwebs. "I don't."

I couldn't blame her. Between first Cheryl ransacking it and now the police, her apartment probably seemed to her more like someplace she didn't belong than someplace she did. So I left her at Ryan's and drove home.

My house was dark, but I could see all the lights on down at Matt's. I didn't particularly want to be alone, especially since Matt would have Latte down with him, so I grabbed my bag from the trunk where it had thankfully been protected from the smoke smell and made my way across the lawn of the empty house between us and over to his house.

As soon as I opened the door, I could hear the sound of the Boston Bruins game coming from the living room. Not wanting to come between a man and his hockey and knowing that I needed a change of clothes and a shower anyway, I just called out to Matt. "Don't mind me! I'm just going to strip so I can wash my clothes and then jump in the shower. I'll come see you when I don't reek like an ashtray."

There was a long pause as I pulled off my coat—dry clean only, unfortunately—and then the sweater I had on as my top layer.

"Uh, Franny? You may not want to do that," Matt called back just as I pulled my thin long sleeve shirt up over my head.

Where I was standing was just out of view of the couch where I assumed Matt was sitting, but to get to the laundry room to wash my clothes, I would have to walk in full view of the living room. I poked my head around the corner and was glad Matt had stopped me when he did.

"Hey Franny," Mike said, the smile on his face somewhere between uncomfortable and amused.

"Hey," I replied, torn between being polite and realizing that I'd almost paraded in front of him naked. As it was, I knew my tank top was see-through, but hoped he couldn't tell that. "I'll just go get a shower first and throw my clothes in the washer later then." I gathered up the shirts I'd dropped on the floor and carried them into Matt's bedroom, making sure I shut the door behind me. I breathed a sigh of relief that I had managed to avoid an utterly mortifying experience.

After I'd scrubbed myself head to toe twice in the fruitiest-smelling body wash I could find—which was mine, not Matt's—and washed my hair three times, I reluctantly got out of the shower. I'd never before realized what a luxury warm *and* good-smelling was. I wrapped my hair up into a bun, got dressed in my favorite old sweatshirt and sweatpants of Matt's, tossed my clothes in the washer with as much detergent and fabric softener as I could, and went out into the living room.

Like typical men, Matt and Mike sat at opposite ends of the couch, as far apart as they could possibly be. I gave Matt a quick kiss.

"Either of you need a refill? What're you drinking?" I asked, heading to the kitchen in search of a beverage.

"Beer," Matt called.

"Water for me," Mike said. Then, lower, and obviously only to Matt, "Gotta drive home, man."

I grabbed a bottle of water for Mike, a beer for Matt, and poured myself a glass of wine. Walking back into the living room, I momentarily considered plopping down between them on the couch, but decided on a chair instead. I wasn't exactly a big hockey fan anyway, although if I was, the Bruins would be my team. Latte immediately came over from where he was laying at Matt's feet and laid down at mine.

"So how'd it go?" Matt asked.

"Cheryl had some interesting friends," I said, sliding off the chair and onto the floor so I could pet Latte.

"Any particularly murderous ones?"

"I don't know. Maybe." Something had been tickling at the back of my mind since we left Boston, but I couldn't put my finger on it.

"Oh yeah? Like who?"

Before I could say anything, Mike interrupted. "You guys know I'm still a cop, right? This may not be my case, but I still work for the department."

"Oh good!" I replied. "Then maybe you can tell Phillips some of my theories." I took a deep breath like I was about to launch into a list.

"I don't think Dick Phillips is interested in anything I have to say."

"Maybe there's someone else you can tell. Like the Chief? Maybe if he heard your theories—"

"You mean your theories?" Mike asked with a smile on his face. Whether it was the Bruins, or Matt's company, or whatever he'd been drinking before I got there, Mike seemed like he was in a good mood. It made me happy, especially since he'd been so miserable for the last month or so.

"Well, yeah."

Mike shook his head.

Latte wiggled and whined a little at my feet.

"I'll take him out," Matt said, hopping up more quickly than he ever had. "Let you two sort this out on your own." Latte followed him to the back door without any hesitation.

I waited until it closed and then looked at Mike. "How bad is it?" I asked quietly.

He sighed. "Bad." He looked at his water bottle

and giggled it a little in his hand. "If I could tell you more—"

"Mike, come on. It's Sammy we're talking about here."

"I know. That's why it's hard."

"Hard to deal with the thought of her going to jail for a crime she didn't commit? Yeah, I know."

"Franny—"

"If you think she did it, then you need to tell me and you need to tell me why. If you don't, then why not tell me whatever it is? You're not going to keep a secret if it could save Sammy, are you?"

Mike's face was anguished. "Franny, it's my job—" He stopped. "I've already lost the Chief's confidence. If he finds out I was running around town, telling people details of a case—"

"A case against your friend. One that you know is wrong." My voice was quiet. I understood what he was feeling. I couldn't blame him if he didn't want to endanger his job. But it was Sammy we were talking about.

He stared at the water bottle. "My family— Sandra—I've already ruined that. The police force is all I have left." The plastic of the water bottle crinkled in his hands. His eyes closed for a long few seconds. He looked up at me. "I may as well torpedo that too."

It wasn't excitement I felt. It was sadness. I was grateful that he was going to help me—help Sammy

—but I couldn't help but be heartbroken over the reason why.

He put the water bottle down next to him, his face back to its typical no-nonsense police detective expression. "The crime lab didn't find any fingerprints on the body or any other DNA. Given how cold it was that night, though, it doesn't surprise me. Gloves make sense not just to disguise evidence, but also just to keep your fingers from freezing off. Aside from Sammy's DNA and the small-size handprints around the victim's neck, there's no other physical evidence. It's all highly circumstantial. Knowing Sammy, there are easy explanations for all of it. There's no denying Cheryl was in Sammy's apartment—that's where she picked up Sammy's DNA. Lots of people have small hands." He took a deep breath. "If I didn't know Sammy though—I'd probably believe it too."

"Has Phillips looked into Cheryl's background at *all*? I mean, I just spent a day talking to people and—"

"You don't go looking for more suspects if you already have a good one just for the sake of having more. Phillips talked to several of Cheryl's friends and searched her apartment in Plymouth. Nothing was a red flag for him."

"Does he know that Cheryl stole two hundred dollars from her mother less than a week before she was killed? And that Cheryl's mother used to come to

Cape Bay as a child? And her alibi for New Year's Eve is weak."

One corner of Mike's mouth twisted up in a near-smile. "Her alibi is corroborated by the Boston Police who were called to her apartment for a noise complaint at one a.m. There's no way she could have been here to kill Cheryl at the right time."

I swore softly under my breath.

The back door opened and Matt and Latte burst in. "Geez Louise it's cold out there!" he said, making me laugh.

"Geez Louise?"

"It's so cold I've reverted to swearing like a little kid. That's how cold it is." He went and stood in front of the fireplace, holding his hands out to warm them.

A whistle sounded from the TV and Mike scooted forward on the couch. "Looks like it's time for me to go."

I looked at the TV and realized that the game was over.

"You okay to drive, man?" Matt asked.

Mike quirked up an eyebrow. "I nursed one beer all night."

"What? You kept getting up to get another one."

"I kept getting up to get *you* another one. I learned a long time ago that if you keep topping off everyone else's glass, they assume you're topping off your own as well."

Matt stood there, looking confused.

Mike grinned and slapped him on the back. "Thanks for inviting me over. I'll see you." He came over and gave me a hug. "Keep thinking, Franny," he whispered.

"Let me know if you think of anything else," I whispered back.

He rubbed Latte on the head and made his way to the door. "Bye guys!"

I stared after him.

"What?" Matt asked.

"It's not just Sammy I have to solve this for. I have to do it for Mike, too."

Chapter 21

THAT NIGHT, I had the strangest dream. At least what I could remember of it was strange, though I couldn't imagine how it would be anything but strange given what I remembered. It was just hands and eggnog. Small hands, specifically. The small hands poured eggnog, they held eggnog, at one point they even dipped themselves into eggnog. The hands weren't attached to anything either. Just disembodied hands playing with eggnog. It was very weird.

The dream didn't help the strange feeling I had tickling in the back of my head—the feeling that I was missing something, that there was something I'd overlooked. It had to do with something someone had said, but I couldn't figure out what it was. I had a feeling it was important though and that if I could figure it out, it would solve the whole case. But I couldn't figure it out. Thinking about it wasn't helping, so I decided to try not thinking about it and went in to the café.

It was closed when I got there, which didn't surprise me. I'd told Sammy she only needed to come to work if she felt like it, and I knew that Rhonda had other commitments that kept her from being able to work the range of hours Sammy and I usually did. Under any other circumstances, I would have felt compelled to make sure I kept the café open its regular hours, but these were far from regular circumstances.

I was a little worried about the state the café would be in when I got there, but I was pleasantly surprised to see that everything was neat and tidy. Not that I thought Rhonda would have left it a pig sty, but I knew that with limited hours, some things could get overlooked. I flipped the open/closed sign on the door around to open, and got to work catching up.

Rhonda had been kind enough to keep a list of the things we were running low on, so I sat down to start working on the ordering. I'd only been sitting for a minute or two when I heard the bell over the door jingle. I was surprised someone had found us open so quickly.

I served that customer, then another and another. Apparently people had missed us. Or at least that was part of why people were coming in.

A couple of young women who looked like they were on their lunch break came in and ordered salads and sandwiches. I suggested they go find a table while I got everything ready. I was walking up to them when I heard one whisper, "Is that her?"

"I don't think so. I'm pretty sure she has blonde hair. And she's younger."

"Have you seen her?"

"No, but I'm trying not to look obvious."

I slammed the plates down on the table. Both girls jumped. "I'm sorry," I said coldly. "I forgot that these were to-go orders. I'll go get a bag for you." I turned on my heel and walked back behind the counter, returning with a bag. Then I stood there and stared at them as they put their lunches in the bag and sheepishly walked away.

I wished I could have said that they were the only people who came in hoping to get a glimpse of the accused murderer, but they weren't. Most of them I managed to silence with a look, but there were a couple of other tables that I had to encourage to leave more quickly than they'd planned. One particularly winning young man snidely said over his shoulder as he walked out, "Well, I didn't really want food made by a murderer anyway."

It took all the strength I had in me not to close the café right then and there. It didn't matter if Sammy was working or not. They were being rude with their gawking and whispering, and I didn't care if they never came back.

No, it was someone else who made me close the

café down for the day. She was a supposedly well-meaning middle aged woman from some local women's group or other who I suspected actually just wanted to stoke drama. She came in nice enough, ordered her coffee and a cupcake, then sat to eat it. She looked around with a pleasant look on her face that, even after the day I'd had, I totally bought into. So when she came up to me on her way out, I didn't think anything of it.

"Fran, is that right?" she said.

"Yup, that's me!" I replied cheerfully.

"I'm Marla, from the Ladies of Cape Bay. You've heard of us?"

"No, I haven't actually. What do you do?"

"Oh, we're just a group of local women who work together for the betterment of Cape Bay and its residents."

"That sounds nice," I said, picking up some plates from a table next to me.

"Yes, well, we heard about Sammy who works here and those awful charges against her."

That should have been my first—or fifth—warning, but it wasn't. Or at least I didn't pick up on it.

"The ladies appointed me as our emissary to come here and let you know that if, God forbid, poor Sammy ends up in prison over this whole thing, we want to be the first to send her a care package. So I do hope you'll let us know exactly how to do that when the time comes. *If*, I mean! If the time comes."

I stared at her for a long time. "You want to be the first to send her a care package," I repeated.

"Yes, exactly! We don't want her to be languishing away in that awful place without knowing that people on the outside are thinking about her."

"She hasn't been arrested or charged with anything and you're already planning to send her a care package."

"Yes! Isn't it wonderful—"

"Get out," I said through clenched teeth.

"I'm sorry, what was that—"

"Get. Out!" I said, louder this time.

"Well, that's not very—"

"Get out!" I yelled, slamming the plates I was holding down on the table I'd just picked them up from. "Get out. All of you! I'm tired of you whispering about Sammy like no one can hear you. I can hear you. And you need to get out. Now! All of you!"

People gradually began to stand up and make their way to the door. A couple of regulars who hadn't said a word about Sammy beyond asking me to let her know they were thinking of her looked at me. "Yes, I'm sorry, you too. I just can't—" Decent people that they were, they got up and left quietly, one of them leaving a large tip on the table that I would set aside for Sammy. Another regular touched my arm gently as she walked by. I tried to smile at her, but it didn't work.

When the last person had filed out, I locked the

door behind them and flipped the sign around to "Closed." Then I went in the back room, sank down to the floor, and cried.

That night, I confided in Matt about what had happened that day at the café and all my worries about the case. As usual, he was encouraging and supportive, but I was still frustrated.

"You know it's not your job to solve it, right, Franny?" he asked.

"Well, yes, but someone has to and the police certainly aren't doing it. Maybe if the Chief had left Mike on the case… "

"'Maybe' doesn't change anything."

"No, and it doesn't get Sammy off the hook either," I said sullenly.

Matt scooted over next to me on the couch and put his arm around me. "I know you're worried about her," he said. "But you have to have faith in the justice system and that an innocent person won't go to jail."

"That's easy for you to say. It's not your friend who's being investigated for murder."

"True," he said and pulled me closer to him. He kissed me on the temple. "You thought about this the whole time you were at the café today, didn't you?"

"Yes! Because I feel like I'm so close! I feel like the answer is right there in front of me and I just can't see it because . . . because . . . because I don't know why. I just can't! I just can't figure it out. It should be so easy! Why am I so terrible at it?"

"Terrible at solving a murder case?"

"Yes!"

"Solving a murder case when the police detective who has been hired specifically to solve this case hasn't solved it either?"

"Yes!"

"You know how ridiculous that sounds, right?"

"Yes," I admitted reluctantly. "It doesn't make me feel any better though."

He ran his fingers through my hair. "Would it make you feel better if I reminded you that you *have* solved a murder case or two before?"

"No," I pouted.

"Because those weren't this one?"

"Yes."

He brushed his fingers against my neck. "You know you don't have to be perfect, don't you Franny?"

"Yes, but I don't like it."

He smiled and kissed me on the nose. "You thought about this all day at the café today, didn't you?"

"Yes, except for when I was fending off gossiping old biddies."

"You know what I think?"

"That the New England Patriots are the greatest football team ever in the history of the sport?"

He grinned. "Aside from that."

"No, what?"

"I'm not saying this just because you're my girlfriend and you're the most beautiful girl in the world and I hate to see your forehead all wrinkled up like that—"

I wrinkled my forehead even more.

"I think you need to try to stop thinking about it for a little while. I know that's easier said than done, but I'm pretty sure that it's been scientifically proven that you can solve problems better when you think about something else for a while."

"Scientifically proven?" I asked, looking into his warm brown eyes.

"Scientifically," he repeated. The corners of his eyes crinkled. He brushed his lips against mine. "Do you think you could try that? Think about something else for a little while?"

"I don't know," I replied playfully. "Did you have something else in mind?"

"Oh, I can think of a thing or two," he said and kissed me again.

Chapter 22

I WAS ALONE in the café late the next day. Business had been slow, but that was to be expected when no one knew whether or not we'd be open at any given time. Normally that would stress me out, especially since I knew that if I had bothered to do my books for the year so far, they'd look like I'd run out of black pen and just decided to use red. But I had more important things on my mind. And so, of course, did Sammy.

I was frustrated with myself and, to be honest, a little angry. I felt like I should have had the case all figured out by now. I'd talked to so many people in Plymouth and in Cape Bay—even up in Boston. I felt like the answer was right there, like it was on the tip of my tongue, but I just couldn't figure it out. And every time I tried to think it through, it was like it was further away than when I didn't think about it. I wanted to give up, but I couldn't. I needed to solve the case. For Sammy. And for Mike.

It was already getting dark outside even though it was barely four o'clock. No wonder people got depressed in the winter. It was never light out. I thought about closing up for the night, even though I knew I really shouldn't. There was usually a wave of customers a little after five, as people stopped in on their way home from work. But I was tired—physically, mentally, emotionally tired—and the café was cleaner than it had probably ever been since I'd spent most of the customer-free day scrubbing every visible surface. I'd even run a wet rag over the exposed brick wall. It didn't seem to have much effect.

I cast one more look outside. The street and sidewalk were empty. Not surprising since it was freezing cold outside. I realized it was entirely possible that I could keep the café open for another two hours and not have a single customer. Why should I do that? Why, when I could go home to my dog and my boyfriend (who wasn't home from work yet, but would be eventually), and sit on the couch in front of a roaring fire with a nice glass of wine? Why indeed?

I went to the immaculately cleaned and organized back room to grab my coat and handbag. Just as I was checking to make sure the back door was locked, I heard a little jingle from the front. Instead of being happy about finally having a customer, my first reaction was to be annoyed that I'd have to clean up all

over again after whoever it was left. So I made a deci-
sion that would probably have my grandparents
rolling over in their graves. I was going to tell the
customer that we were closed and send them away.
"Sorry Nonna. Sorry Nonno," I whispered. Fully
bundled up for the cold, I went out to break the news
to my customer.

It was Mike.

"Oh! Hey!" I said.

"You closing up?"

"Yeah, I was going to. It's been slow today, so I
figured I may as well. But if you want something, I'll
make it for you."

Mike hesitated with a guilty look on his face.
"Well, I—"

"Oh, sit down!" I said. He made a move towards
one of the tables. "No, in the back. I'm closing up
anyway."

I went to the front door and locked it, then started
a pot of coffee for Mike and an espresso for me. At
least I could use a to-go cup for him and my own
travel mug for myself so the coffee pot would be the
only thing that needed to be cleaned.

When our drinks were ready, I took them to the
back room and shut the door to hide the light from
anyone passing by on the street. Knowing my
customers, they'd assume a light in the back meant we
were open even if the sign on the door said we were
closed.

I passed Mike his cup and sat down across from him. "You just looking for a cup of coffee or did you have another reason for stopping by?"

Mike looked guilty again. He looked down at his coffee.

I waited.

"It's not good news," he said.

My stomach dropped.

"Phillips is going to the district attorney for an arrest warrant by the end of the week."

I wanted to throw up. Then I thought of something. "But it's Wednesday."

Mike nodded. "He didn't say it, but my guess would be that he's planning to arrest her Friday night after five so she has to spend the weekend in jail before she can see a judge to be arraigned."

"Are you serious?"

"A nice, long weekend in jail is a good way to get someone to confess. Promise them leniency if they just tell you the truth. It's a dirty move, but it works."

I thought for a second and realized that Mike didn't just mean that two days in jail would seem long. This weekend actually was a long weekend. If Sammy was arrested Friday night, she'd spend three whole days in jail before the courts reopened. "What are we going to do?" I whispered.

"Figure out who killed her yet?"

"No, have you?" I retorted a little more harshly

than I intended. "Sorry," I muttered. "That wasn't nice."

"I'm not easily offended." Mike took a long drink from his coffee cup. "The way I figure it, it wasn't Sammy. We know she wouldn't have done it. I don't think it was random. Strangling is too personal. If you're going to kill someone at random, you don't strangle them. It's too up close and personal. This was someone who knew her and wanted her dead."

"And do you know who that person is?"

He chuckled. "Wouldn't be sitting here if I did."

We each sat silently, staring at our drinks.

"It had to be someone here in town or someone who knew she'd be here," Mike said after a few minutes.

"So, anyone who knew her?"

"Yeah, pretty much." He drank his coffee. "Who could it be here in town?"

I thought for a minute, then shrugged. "No one, really. Not that I can think of. It wasn't Sammy. It couldn't have been Ryan."

"Why not?" Mike asked quickly.

"You think it was Ryan?"

"Just answer the question."

"Because, one, I don't think he would kill someone, and, two, have you seen his hands? They're enormous!"

Mike nodded and almost smiled. "That's what I

wanted to hear. You using the evidence. Now, who else?"

"The only other people who knew her at all or knew she was in town are me and you. I didn't do it. Did you?"

"Life's in the toilet enough as it is. I don't need to kill anyone to make it worse. Also—" He held up his hands. Given that his palm could practically cover my entire face, I didn't think they could be mistaken for being small.

"So that's it—that's everyone in town. Except Bonnie. But Bonnie had never met her before she offered to let her stay at her place."

"Are you sure? Sounds a little strange letting someone you've never met stay at your house."

"Have you met Bonnie? I don't think it would occur to her that anything bad could happen. She's an incredibly sweet person."

Mike nodded but didn't look convinced.

"Besides, she's from Georgia and she went to college in Providence before she moved here. Cheryl only ever lived in Plymouth. There's no connection there."

"Okay, who else?"

I had thought long and hard over everyone Sammy and I had talked to on our road trip. The vast majority of them, I had written off. They weren't killers, or their hands were too big, or they actually had a good alibi. "I'm still not convinced it wasn't her mother."

"I told you, the police were at her apartment that night. She couldn't have come down here."

"Did the police actually talk to her? Did they see her? Did they *know* it was her?"

Mike looked at me skeptically. "I'm not staking my career on her. If you want to go to Phillips and try to sell him on it, I won't stop you."

Since I wasn't exactly keen on the idea of convincing Phillips of anything, I kept going. Besides, my list wasn't much longer. "The only other person who stands out is this guy Chris Miller. He broke up with his girlfriend for Cheryl and then Cheryl dumped him almost right away. His girlfriend killed herself."

Mike let out a low whistle. "Well, there's a motive. But he's a guy." Mike held up his hands and wiggled his fingers.

"He's a very small guy. Short. Petit. Small hands."

Mike nodded. "So is he your guy?"

"What do you think?"

"I don't know, Franny. I haven't met him. What does your gut tell you?"

I thought for a moment. When I thought back to our conversation, I saw only sadness, not homicidal rage. But I kept thinking of him. "I don't know."

"Fair enough. But you need to listen for it. That's how you'll know. Your gut will tell you."

I thought for a moment. I had an idea, but I wasn't sure about it. What I was sure about was that we didn't have much time. We had—maybe—forty-eight hours before Phillips would arrest Sammy. It was now or never. Do or die. I wasn't sure who killed Cheryl, but I knew that if I wanted to save Sammy, there was only one thing I could do.

"If you hear a murder confession, you can arrest that person without a warrant, right?" I asked Mike.

He nodded slowly. "You're not about to confess are you, Fran? Because if you are, I'm going to advise against it. Go get a lawyer. Call Giorgio DiGiorgio."

I shook my head. "No, I'm not going to confess!"

"Then what?" Mike looked at me expectantly.

"Can you be here tomorrow night at five?"

Chapter 23

I SPENT the next couple of hours on the phone, calling people and asking them to come to the café at five o'clock the next day. Most of them agreed readily —a few were a little harder to convince, but in the end, I got everyone I really wanted to be there to agree to come. I had initially wavered between inviting everyone I talked to or just a smaller group, but I decided on the smaller group. Inviting everyone would have just been a distraction technique, and while it was meant to distract my invitees, I was afraid it would distract me also. The smaller group would be better.

I went home that night and filled Matt in on my plan. He was skeptical, but I managed to convince him. Or at least convince him to be supportive and go along with it for my sake.

I slept surprisingly well that night. I would have

thought that the anticipation would keep me awake, but it seemed that my psyche was more comforted by the fact that, with any luck, this would be over soon. Still, I dreamt of eggnog and small hands. Small hands holding eggnog. Small hands pointing at eggnog. Sometimes they were comically small, like little doll hands holding a giant jug of eggnog. My subconscious was trying to tell me something, but I didn't know what. I would have liked it if it could have just shown me who the murderer was, but maybe it wasn't too sure of it either. Either that or it thought coming up with the answer in a dream would be too cliché. Of course, dreaming of clues was too.

I woke up without my alarm the next morning. For a moment, I just laid there, then I remembered. Today was the day. I got out of bed and breezed through my morning routine. Shower, clothes, hair, makeup, make myself a big cup of coffee, take Latte for a walk. When everything was done, I headed to the café.

I had no intention of opening it. Not to customers, anyway. I wanted everything to be perfect for that night, and I wanted plenty of time to do it. I dragged all the tables and chairs out of their normal positions. The tables I lined up against the wall, the chairs I arranged in a circle. I made two big batches of eggnog. I wanted to make sure I had more than enough for the night. It wasn't quite as good as

Bonnie's, but it would do. There was no alcohol in it, of course. I didn't want things getting out of hand.

I arranged two big platters of snacks. Cupcakes, tiramisu, ladyfingers, cookies—an assortment of all the things we sold. Snacks gave people something to do with their hands. Sugar made them happy. I laid everything out on the counter along with some cups, plates, and napkins, and stood back to admire my handiwork. It had taken me most of the day, but I was happy with the way it looked.

I went in the back to sit down for a few minutes and collect my thoughts. I made some notes and read over them a few dozen times. I wanted it memorized. I didn't want to have to refer to my notes during such an important moment.

At four-forty-five, I unlocked the front door. I took down the open/closed sign. I didn't want anyone to use the sign saying "closed" as an excuse for why they didn't come. And I certainly didn't want anyone to think we were open.

Five minutes later, I started a pot of coffee. I would offer everyone a coffee drink, but I knew Mike would just want a plain, black, drip coffee, so wanted to go ahead and get it started. While my back was turned, I heard the bell over the door jingle. My heart pounded. I wasn't ready!

I turned around and saw it was Mrs. D'Angelo, our friendly town busybody. She had a habit of appearing just when I wanted to see her least, but this was a new level of bad timing.

"Hi Mrs. D'Angelo! I'm sorry, we're actually closed right now! I'm hosting a meeting—"

"No, no, Francesca, dear. I'm not here for one of your little drinks. I'm just here to drop something off for Bonnie!"

"For Bonnie? Bonnie Harmon?"

"Yes, yes, she *is* going to be here tonight, isn't she? Lovely girl. We're *so* glad she moved to town!" Mrs. D'Angelo breezed around the counter as she tended to do. Fortunately, she had a stack of papers in one hand and a box in the other, so she didn't have any hands free to use to grasp onto my arm with her long, sharp red nails. Her hands being full didn't stop her heavy floral perfume from assaulting me though. That did it on its own.

"How did you know Bonnie was going to be here tonight?" I asked. It probably wasn't the most necessary question, but it was the one that sprang first to my mind.

"Oh, she told us this morning at the Genealogy Society meeting!"

"The Genealogy Society meeting?" I repeated. I knew Mrs. D'Angelo was involved with the town's Genealogy Society—everyone did, she made sure of it —but I was surprised to hear that Bonnie was, too.

"Yes! She's been coming to our meetings since she moved to town. Lovely girl, just lovely. And with that darling accent! Her mother's people are from up here, you know. That's why she moved to Plymouth. Anyway, these are the documents she requested—"

"Wait, Plymouth? No, Bonnie moved here from Providence." I was sure it was Providence because she said she'd gone to the Rhode Island School of Design and then stayed in town.

"Well, yes, after stopping in Plymouth for a few years. Anyway, these are the documents—"

"*Plymouth*," I repeated. "You're sure she lived in *Plymouth*?"

Mrs. D'Angelo looked at me like I'd lost my mind. And maybe I had. "Yes, Francesca. I'm sure she lived in Plymouth. We spoke specifically about how she went to see Plymouth Rock every Thanksgiving because she wanted to be reminded of the struggles her ancestors went through when they first came here. Now these documents—"

Mrs. D'Angelo kept talking, but I didn't hear any of it. My mind was reeling. If Bonnie had moved from Plymouth instead of Providence, that could— that could change everything. But did it? Did it make sense? My mind raced through the possibilities. I needed to talk to Sammy. I needed to ask her—

"You'll tell her that, won't you Francesca? It's very important that she understands."

"What?" I suddenly realized that whatever Mrs. D'Angelo was saying needed a response. "Yes, of course. Of course I will."

"Excellent! Now I'll just put these things here and then I have to run! The Ladies' Auxiliary's first Christmas committee meeting is tonight and if I don't leave now, I'll be late!"

"Christmas committee? It's the second week in January."

"Yes, I know! We're already so behind!" Mrs. D'Angelo dropped her papers on the counter and made her way over to the door. "Thank you for passing those things along, Francesca!" And she was out the door.

I was still standing there, thinking over what she'd said when the door opened again. It was Mike. "Oh, thank goodness!"

I ran over to him and quickly gave him a rundown of what I expected to happen that night. I pointed out where I planned for everyone to sit and left it up to him to decide where he wanted to position himself. He asked a few questions, but agreed to my overall plan. He decided to sit by the door. I was just done talking to him when Ryan and Sammy came in. I told Ryan where to sit and grabbed Sammy.

I pulled her off to the side and whispered a question in her ear.

She nodded.

I whispered another question.

She thought for a moment and nodded again, whispering her reply.

"Now this is the important one," I said, and whispered the last question.

Sammy looked bewildered for a second, then thoughtful. Her lips twitched and I could tell she was going over every word of the conversation we'd had before. Finally, she shook her head. "No," she said slowly, and repeated back the part of the conversation I'd asked about.

I nodded and started to walk away. "Oh, sit next to Ryan. His left side, not his right."

Sammy looked at me like I was crazy, but sat where I told her. Matt came in a moment later and I told him where to stand and what I wanted him to do. Chris Miller came in next. I directed him to the chair directly opposite the door, his back to Matt.

Lois came in next, in a waft of stale cigarette smoke that made me miss Mrs. D'Angelo's heavy perfume. I directed her to the seat right between Sammy and Chris.

Several minutes passed without Bonnie arriving. I was starting to get worried when I looked out the door and saw her jogging down the sidewalk. I held the door for her as she rushed in.

"Sorry I'm late!" she said.

"No problem. Take a seat right there, next to Ryan," I told her.

I glanced at Matt as Bonnie hesitated for a moment, then took her seat. Matt nodded his head so slightly that I wouldn't have noticed if I hadn't been looking for it. I looked at Sammy. Her eyes widened for a second, then she nodded. I looked at Mike. He gave me a look that I read as doubtful but impressed and nodded also.

So that was it. I took a deep breath.

I smiled and walked over to one of the two remaining empty chairs.

"Okay, so now that everybody's here, let's get started."

Chapter 24

"I ASKED you all here today because of one, unfortunate thing that links us all. I'm sure I don't need to tell any of you that that unfortunate thing is Cheryl's death. Each of us here was affected by Cheryl in some way."

I started on my right.

"You, Chris, dated Cheryl. Once a few years ago, and then again earlier this year."

I looked at Lois.

"You, Lois, were Cheryl's mother. First of all, we all want to express our sincere condolences for your loss."

Lois rolled her eyes.

"We know that you and Cheryl had a contentious relationship and that she even stole two hundred dollars from you a couple of weeks ago. Even so, we know how painful this time must be for you and we appreciate you coming tonight."

She looked around, then grabbed a cookie from the platter behind her.

I skipped over Sammy.

"Ryan, you dated Cheryl back when you were in high school and recently ran into her here in town."

Ryan looked back at me blankly. He didn't seem to be sure what to think of the little production I had going on.

I looked between Sammy and Bonnie, then smiled at Sammy.

"Sammy, you received a series of harassing text messages from Cheryl and are currently being investigated by the police for her murder. In fact, if my sources are correct, you're going to be arrested for that tomorrow night."

Sammy gasped and looked like she was going to throw up. Ryan, despite his obvious shock, immediately leaned over and cradled her to his chest. Bonnie and Chris looked between me and Sammy, frozen like deer in the headlights. Matt looked surprised, and Lois looked like she couldn't have cared less. I avoided looking at Mike because I knew he would be none too happy with me for sharing that information. But it was my trump card and I had to play it. I felt bad for springing it on Sammy like that, but her reaction had to be real.

I looked at each of my guests in turn, as emotionless as I could be.

We waited as Ryan whispered in Sammy's ear, trying his best to calm her down. After what seemed like an eternity, he succeeded. At least enough for me to resume.

I looked at Bonnie.

"And you, Bonnie—"

I paused and looked around the circle again.

"You, Bonnie, graciously took Cheryl into your home even though—"

I stopped to clear my throat.

"Excuse me! Even though she was a total stranger."

I enunciated those words carefully.

"Not many people would do that. It's a very, very kind thing for you to have done."

I looked around again, letting my words sink in. The café was quiet except for Sammy's sniffles.

I crossed my legs and leaned back in my chair.

"Now, the problem is, Sammy didn't kill Cheryl. She's about to go to jail for it, but she didn't kill her."

I paused again.

"What's worse is—"

More looking around the room.

"What's worse is that someone in this room did kill her, just not Sammy."

I let it sink in. I looked from one person to the next in search of a reaction.

"One of you is going to let Sammy go to jail for a crime she didn't commit."

I uncrossed my legs and recrossed them the other way. Anything to create tension.

"Now, I know it wasn't Lois."

I didn't know that an hour ago, but I did now.

"And I'm not saying that because she was Cheryl's mother or because she has a pretty airtight alibi."

I wanted to glance over at Mike, but I was afraid he was still seething over my announcing Sammy was going to be arrested.

"I'm saying that because all facts, all the evidence, everything I've learned from everyone I've talked to about this case, show that it's someone else. And if we know it's not Sammy or Lois, and we know it's not Ryan, that means it's—"

I looked to my left.

"It's you, Bonnie. *Or*—"

I looked to my right.

"Or it's you, Chris."

I leaned forward and put my elbows on my knees, folding my hands in front of me.

"Now the thing I didn't know an hour ago, not even half an hour ago, if I'm being honest, is that Bonnie and Chris here know each other. They know each other pretty well. In fact, they just broke up a few months ago."

Chris and Bonnie looked uncomfortable. Sammy

had suddenly stopped crying and was staring at me in shock.

"See, what threw me off, what took me so long to figure it out, was that Bonnie never told me that she moved here from Plymouth. She let me think she moved from Providence. And Chris, Chris kept calling his girlfriend "B." And in my head, I heard B-E-A, not just the letter B. But the letter B is what he meant. So it took me a while to figure it out. And on top of that, Chris said his girlfriend was gone. And the way he said it and the way he cried and made it sound like she was never coming back, well, Sammy and I thought she was dead. We thought she killed herself. But she didn't. No, she came to Cape Bay, and that is far from killing herself.

"So Chris and Bonnie both, well, didn't quite lie, but definitely kept some things from me and Sammy. And I guess from the police since they didn't catch on either. But Mrs. D'Angelo—"

I smiled at Bonnie and wagged a finger.

"Mrs. D'Angelo blew your cover. And as soon as she did that, I knew. I knew that the great eggnog Chris kept going on about was the same as the great eggnog I had at Bonnie's. I knew. Now, the thing is, you both have a motive for murder. Chris, you thought you were going to marry Bonnie until Cheryl came along and convinced you to blow up your relationship for her, then left you after a couple of weeks. And Bonnie, well, it's the same thing but from the other side. You both have a motive. But only one of you did it."

I looked down at my hands.

"Only one of you."

The problem was, I still didn't know which one of them it was. Chris or Bonnie, Bonnie or Chris. It could be either one. But it could only be one. I took a deep breath and listened for my gut.

Chapter 25

"IT WAS ME!" Chris said, jumping up from his chair.

I looked up, startled, but relieved. My gut hadn't spoken to me yet, and I hadn't been sure what I was going to say next. Bonnie did though.

"Oh shut up, Chris! And sit down," she said from her chair. "You know you didn't kill her and some last minute heroic claim that you did isn't going to fix anything between us. Not like it would matter anyway since if you convince the police that you're guilty, you're going to jail anyway."

Everyone in the room stared at Bonnie.

"Chris is lying. I did it. I killed Cheryl."

Out of the corner of my eye, I noticed Mike stand up a little straighter.

"And it wasn't because of you either, you idiot," Bonnie said. "It was because of her." She looked at Sammy. "That poor girl. I saw what Cheryl was doing to her." She looked at me. "That's why I invited her to stay with me. I saw her out on the street one day, staring into this place, so I struck up a conversation. She didn't even recognize me. She ruined my life and she didn't even recognize me! So I saw my chance. I invited her to stay with me. She let on that she was here to get an old boyfriend back from the girl he was with now. Well, I wasn't gonna stand for that. She followed Sammy and I followed her. That night, New Year's Eve, I followed her to your house." She looked at me. I got chills realizing that they'd been there. "And then I followed her over to Sammy's apartment and back to Fran's house. She followed Ryan and Sammy back to his house, and I followed her. She was watching them. Through the window. And I just—I knew she wouldn't let that girl rest until she'd ruined her relationship just like she ruined mine. There was only one way to stop her."

"You killed her," I said softly.

Bonnie tipped her chin up at me. "Yes, I did. I walked up behind her and tapped her on the shoulder. When she turned around, I asked her if she knew who I was. And then I told her. I told her how she ruined my life. And you know what? I did think about killing myself. But that would have been letting her win. And instead, I won. She laughed in my face when I told her who I was. And so I wrapped my hands around her stupid little neck and I squeezed until she was dead. And I'm not sorry either. I'm sorry

I didn't confess earlier, Sammy, that I put you through all that. I never thought they'd actually arrest you. But I'm not sorry I killed Cheryl."

Now I was brave enough to look at Mike. He bent his head and mimed tipping his cap to me, then walked over behind Bonnie.

"Bonnie Harmon, I need you to stand up for me."

Bonnie looked over her shoulder and sighed. She stood and faced Mike, putting her arms out with her wrists together.

"Behind your back, please," he said softly.

She turned around and faced us again as he cuffed her. Her chin was raised defiantly in the air, but there was also a single tear running down her cheek.

Chapter 26

IT WAS hours later that I was finally sitting at home quietly with Matt. After Mike escorted Bonnie out, he'd had another officer come back to take all our statements. And then after Chris and Lois left, Matt, Sammy, Ryan, and I stood around talking for a while. Sammy asked me how I knew, and I had to admit, up until the moment she confessed, I didn't.

But that was earlier. Now, I was at home with Matt and Latte, exactly where I wanted to be.

Matt's arm was slung around my shoulders, his fingers lightly brushing my collarbone. "That was pretty impressive," he said softly, his breath warm against my ear.

"It's like I told Sammy, it was luck, plain and simple."

"I don't believe that." His voice was low and it made me feel all warm and fuzzy inside.

"It's the truth!"

"Maybe, but you still solved the case."

"The case solved itself."

He smiled and brushed his lips against mine. "With a little help from you."

"Just a little," I giggled.

"Mike sounded pretty impressed, too, when he came back to thank you."

"He was just glad he got to make the arrest instead of Phillips."

"So? You solved the crime and got the detective his job back. I'd say you saved the day." He kissed me again. This was getting distracting. Not that I minded. I liked being distracted.

"I wouldn't go as far as saying I saved the day."

"No? Then what would you say?"

I thought for a second. "I'd say I'm actually pretty good at this solving murders thing."

Matt grinned. His lips hovered over mine as he said softly, "Yes, you are, Franny. Yes, you are."

Recipe 1: Homemade Eggnog

Makes 12 servings

Ingredients:

- 12 egg yolks
- 4 cups milk
- 4 cups light cream
- 5 whole cloves
- 2 1/2 cups rum
- 1 1/2 cups sugar
- 2 1/2 tsp vanilla extract
- 1 tsp ground cinnamon
- 1/2 tsp ground nutmeg

In a saucepan over low heat, add milk, cloves, 1/2 tsp vanilla extract, and cinnamon. Bring milk mixture to boil.

In a large bowl, whisk egg yolks and sugar

together until fluffy. Add hot milk mixture in slowly. Pour mixture into the same saucepan. Stir over medium heat for 3 minutes or until thick. Do not boil. Strain to remove cloves. Let cool for an hour.

Still in rum, cream, remaining 2 tsp. vanilla extract, and nutmeg. Refrigerate overnight before serving.

Recipe 2: Eggnog Latte

1 serving

Ingredients:

- 2/3 cup eggnog (see first recipe)
- 2 Tbsp sugar
- 1/2 cup coffee or 2 shots of espresso
- 1/3 cup milk
- optional: pinch of ground nutmeg

Froth eggnog, milk and sugar with espresso machine. If you don't have a machine, you can put the ingredients in a microwavable glass jar with a lid. Shake it for up to a minute until it is frothy, *remove the lid*, and microwave it for up to 45 seconds. Take out the jar— the jar might be hot, so use a cloth. Screw the lid back on and shake it again for up to a minute until it is frothy again. *Remove the lid* again, put the glass jar back in the microwave for up to 45 seconds. Watch the jar so the bubbles don't overflow. Stop it if it does.

Add coffee or espresso to jar. Add hot milk, stopping the froth of the milk with a spoon. Add froth on top. Optional: sprinkle on a pinch of ground nutmeg.

About the Author

Harper Lin is the *USA TODAY* bestselling author of 6 cozy mystery series including *The Patisserie Mysteries* and *The Cape Bay Cafe Mysteries*.

When she's not reading or writing mysteries, she loves going to yoga classes, hiking, and hanging out with her family and friends.

www.HarperLin.com

Made in the USA
Middletown, DE
15 April 2018